Worth Dying For

Sydney C. Alix

Illustrated by Bailey R. Alix

ISBN: 979-8-9929435-1-1

MARY HAD NEVER FORGOTTEN THE CONVERSATION THAT THE TWO OF THEM HAD TOGETHER

Table of Contents

Dedication
Acknowledgements
Preface
List of Illustrations

Chapter

Epilogue

Dedication

To my siblings Bailey and Luke, two modern day American patriots, and to my parents, who first taught me to love and cherish my beautiful country, and who inspire me daily as they fight to preserve our God-given freedoms for the next generation.

Acknowledgments

I would like to thank my parents for providing me with such excellent history teachers as William Federer, David Barton, Rick Green, Dinesh D'Souza, and Dave Stotts, all of whom taught me to love history and recognize the importance of knowing and remembering it.

I also want to thank my little sister, Bailey, for being willing to illustrate this book, and helping me with the tedious editing process — I couldn't have written this book without her!

Preface

My hope and prayer is that whoever reads this story will be inspired to truly love and cherish our nation's remarkable and unprecedented history and heritage, and develop an even greater appreciation for the incredible the freedoms that we as Americans enjoy today.

Freedom is not free, and is often only secured at a very high cost. It is also very fragile, and if not guarded and protected, can easily be lost. Many of our forefathers sacrificed everything — even their lives — so that the future generations after them (including you and me) would not have to live under tyranny, and enjoy the freedoms that God intended men to have.

The history of the Alamo is one of the most powerful of such examples in America's history. An incredible story of courage, devotion, fortitude, and sacrifice, may it never be forgotten, and continue to inspire and remind Americans for generations to come that freedom is a sacred inheritance worth fighting, and even dying for.

Illustrations

"I'd read up on the history of our country and I'd become fascinated with the story of the Alamo. To me it represented the fight for freedom, not just in America, but in all countries [16]."

~ John Wayne

Chapter 1

In Which the Characters Are Introduced

It was the beginning of November in 1835, in San Antonio, Texas. Mary Drury, nursing assistant to Doctor Arthur Dopkins, was busy cleaning the medical instruments that the doctor had used that day during his visits to the wounded Texans from the recent San Antonio siege. A young woman of about 20 years of age, she was of medium height, with light brown hair pulled back into a loose bun, and attired in a dark gray dress that, though very plain, did credit to its wearer.

The siege of San Antonio had concluded with the Texans successfully forcing the Mexican army, then commanded by General Cos, to surrender and return across the Rio Grande into Mexico, which for the time being, left all of Texas in their hands [1]. After such a triumphant defeat of the enemy, the future of Texas looked bright and promising, and it seemed as though achieving ultimate victory in the war to secure freedom for Texas was certain. So much change had come about in such a short time, Mary thought to herself, as she worked, recalling all the events that had taken place in both her life, and in the world around her during the past few years.

She thought back to the days of her childhood and life on her family's small farm. It had been located about 20 miles outside of Knoxville, Tennessee, and there she had lived and worked alongside her parents, William and Eliza Drury, and her big brother Benjamin, who was her elder by three years. Life had never been easy for the Drury family; their extreme poverty had forced them to work long, hard hours every day on their farm in order to make ends meet. Despite their hardships, they always managed to be content and simply grateful to be together, as well as for the comfort brought by knowing that God would give them the strength and wisdom they needed to face each day.

Sadly, their quiet life together was not to last for long, for when Mary was about 12 years old, her father was tragically and unexpectedly killed in a farming accident. Somehow, during the difficult days that followed his death, Mary and Ben had managed to both keep the farm going and care for their grieving mother. A year after her husband's sudden death, Eliza Drury was married once again to a bachelor by the name of John Wilkerson, a step that Mary had always believed she had taken in order to provide security for her family. Unfortunately, John Wilkerson had proved to be anything but a support to the Drury family. He liked Eliza and the farm he had gained by marrying her well enough, but he had absolutely no use for Mary and Ben, and his dislike for them had grown more evident with each passing day. For their mother's sake, both children had done everything in their power to please their stepfather, but it was to no avail. In the end, they did their best to keep out of his way, and worked as hard as they could at the jobs he had allotted to them, hoping to minimize his daily outbursts of rage and vexation that brought such great sorrow to their dear mother.

Eliza had never fully recovered from the loss of her first husband, and just two years after his death, she became very ill and died, leaving her children to the tender mercies of their cruel stepfather. John Wilkerson had no intention of being left with the charge of his deceased wife's offspring, and lost no time in selling off the farm, taking the proceeds of the sale for himself, and abandoning Ben and Mary, declaring that they were both plenty old enough to look after themselves. Ben had arranged for transportation to Knoxville with some neighbors, and once they had arrived, immediately set about finding a safe home for Mary. Providentially, they had met Doctor Dopkins, who kindly agreed to allow Mary to come and live with him and his sister in exchange for her housekeeping services. Ben was able to find employment on a farm on the outskirts of Knoxville, and after they were both situated, he and Mary had been able to get on very well for several months.

Eventually, both siblings began to long for their old way of life, and seriously discussed the possibility of relocating. They had both been hearing many reports about Texas, particularly regarding how welcoming and eager the Mexican government was to having foreign settlers immigrate to their land, and inhabit the Texas wilderness.

Little did the two siblings know that this was due to the fact that hardly any of the native Mexican people were willing to risk the dangers the wild wilderness posed, the foremost of which being the aggressive, warring Indian tribes [2]. In an attempt to solve this problem, the Mexican government created enticing incentives such as land grants to encourage Anglo settlers and traders to migrate to Texas. This was done with the hope that the new settlers would both revitalize the struggling economy, and help to control the waring Indian tribes that inhabited the wild Texas territory, terrorizing any who attempted to settle there. One of the first American settlement efforts in Texas was led by a certain Stephen Austin in 1821, who brought over 300 families to settle Texas. In the years that followed, he and others like him continued to bring settlers to the Texas frontier, and it wasn't long before Texas was populated with many successful settlements and an ever-increasing population of Anglo settlers. Many of these settlers were simple, hard-working folk that had left hard lives and difficult circumstances, and had moved to Texas for a fresh start, with the hope of one day transforming the wild frontier into a thriving land [12], [22], [24].

In the early autumn of the year 1828, Ben had decided to travel to Texas with a small company of settlers, and set up a small homestead. Though he knew that such a venture would take some time to complete, he trusted that before too long he could come back for Mary, and that together, they could return to the former life that they so sorely missed. Mary had never forgotten the conversation that the two of them had together just before his departure. "Oh Ben, I don't know how I'm going to stand being separated from you!" she had cried tearfully. "I know Mary," He had answered quietly, "I hardly know how I am going to bear it myself. But you know that I must go if we are ever to have a place of our own again." "I understand, Ben." Mary replied, hastily wiping away her tears. "I just don't know what I am going to do without you. How long do you suppose you will be away?" "Well, I can't rightly say, Sis," Ben said with a sigh, "Tis a long journey from here to Texas, and after I get there, it will take me some time to prepare a home for the both of us. If it were not for the fact that the entire business is so confoundedly dangerous, I wouldn't hesitate to take you with me." "Well," Mary said with an attempt at cheerfulness, "I suppose that the sooner you start, the sooner our separation will be over." "That's right, Mary," Ben answered, "And I am so grateful that God has provided you with such a splendid home with Doctor Dopkins and his sister. They are such kind people, and it will give me great peace of mind to know that you are safe with them." "I too am very thankful, Ben, and I do not wish to seem ungrateful. I just wish I could have some way of being assured of your safety when you are away." At this, Ben had placed his hand gently on her shoulder and met her worried, downcast gaze. "Mary," he said, "Something that I want you to always remember is that no matter how far away I am, or how alone you feel, our Lord will always be with you, as He will also be with me. Whenever you feel anxious or troubled, call out to Him, and He will strengthen you, and give you His perfect peace." "Thank you Ben, I will remember," Mary replied, her eyes filling with tears once again as she met the kind gaze of brother, "It comforts me to know that Someone will also be watching over you as well, wherever you go, and whatever you face." At this, both siblings had embraced each other tightly, taking comfort in this mutual source of strength which they had both learned to lean upon, and which they knew would enable them to withstand the difficult days ahead.

The days following Ben's departure had been quite trying for Mary at first, but Dr. Dopkins and his sister did all that they could to cheer her and make her life with them as happy as they could. In turn, she had proved to be such a wonderful housekeeper that they both often wondered to themselves how they had ever been able to get on before her coming. As Mary spent more and more time with Dr. Dopkins, she developed a very strong interest in his work. He had been quick to observe this as he listened to, and answered all of her eager questions about his patients, and his methods of treating them. It wasn't long before he began taking her with him on his routine visits to his patients, during which she did her best to observe and learn all that she could. She proved to be such a quick study that Dr. Dopkins eventually trained her more formally. This enabled her to be of even greater assistance to him in his work, and after some time, upon realizing how indispensable she had become to him, Dr. Dopkins asked Mary if she would become his full-time nursing assistant, a proposal to which she eagerly assented.

Mary recalled how happy she had been with her new line of work, and how much pleasure Ben's occasional letters afforded her. Soon after his arrival, Ben had secured a position as a ranch hand at a well established Mexican outfit that raised and fattened cattle on the Texas frontier, and drove them back to Mexico to be sold. His eagerness to learn and hard work ethic soon led him to be well accepted by the Mexican vaqueros, several of which befriended him and went on to instruct and accustom him to the duties of ranch life. After over a year of grueling, backbreaking labor, Ben managed to secure a substantial land grant several miles outside of the thriving city of San Antonio, and with the help of several of his new-found friends, set to work at building a small but sturdy ranch house. As the years passed, Ben continued to work, scrape, and save enough money to purchase necessary supplies, and used any spare time to continue work on their homestead. In addition, Mary would send her small earnings from her work to help fund Ben's efforts, and slowly but surely, their dream began to take shape. Mary treasured every one of Ben's letters, in which he was faithful to relate the progress he was making in setting up their little homestead, as well as hopeful plans of his return to come and fetch her to their new home.

As time went on, however, Ben's letters lost their hopeful tune as he began sending her reports of the growing tensions between the Mexican government and the Texas settlers. The number of Anglo settlers in Texas had grown so dramatically that they greatly outnumbered the Mexican population in Texas. Additionally, the widely different cultural and belief systems of the American settlers were having a significant influence on the Mexican population in Texas (i.e. Tejanos). American settlers had come from a nation of freedom, where the government was limited and sought to protect their God-given rights. This was a mindset and way of living that they brought with them to the Texas frontier, and which was quickly embraced by their Tejano neighbors, making them much more wary of the often authoritarian overreach of the Mexican government, and more apt to resist its tyrannical advances. As a result, the Mexican government began to assert its power to bring the Texans under its authority, and stop the advance of their freedom oriented influence upon its people [24]. The first major symptoms of trouble began in 1830, when the governmental structure of Texas was reorganized, and ceased to be friendly and welcoming to the immigrating settlers. Any further Anglo immigration into Texas was quickly shut down, and promised colonial land grants suspended, which were actions that threatened to stifle and suppress the Texas settlements and upend all the Texan's hard earned efforts to establish a thriving civilization in the wild wilderness. Determined to concentrate their authority, the Mexican government went on to impose customs duties and high taxes on the Texans, installed military garrisons across Texas to force the compliance of its citizens, and even arrested and imprisoned many of the colonists without reason or cause [2], [22], [23], [24].

The Mexican government itself was in a near constant state of chaos, for while Mexico had originally established a republican form of government and federal constitution in 1824, this new government had proved to be very unstable and tumultuous. Ultimately in 1833, the newly elected president of Mexico General Santa Anna, decisively seized the reigns of power and quickly transformed the Mexican government, a change that would affect not only all of Mexico, but also its territories, including Texas. Santa Anna, seeking to pattern himself after Napoleon, the recent dictator of Europe, rejected the Mexican Constitution, and after declaring himself to be the dictator of Mexico, he proceeded to order all Mexican citizens to surrender their guns. Multiple Mexican states rebelled against his tyrannical orders, but Santa Anna was quick to crush them by unleashing the military on all who resisted his authority, inciting killings, looting, pillaging, and putting many of his prisoners to the sword. In response to these acts of tyranny, the Texan settlers chose to stand in defense of their rights against Santa Anna and his despotic government. They at first attempted to do so through peaceful means, by entreating the Mexican government to uphold the rights of its citizens and adhere to its original constitution. However, Santa Anna refused to heed their just demands, and instead answered them with still more acts of tyranny [3], even arresting and imprisoning those who attempted to appeal to the Mexican government on behalf of the people of Texas. At last, after multiple failed attempts to resolve their situation peacefully, the Texans recognized the need to take more decisive steps to defend their freedom [22], [24].

As these matters began coming to a head, Ben was forced to inform his sister that he was going to put off his return for her until it was safe to do, something which he feared would not be for quite some time. "I long for the day when I am able to welcome you to our new home," he wrote, "and we are at last able to make our new start in life together, but I cannot return for you in such a time of uncertainty, and with such troubling events on the horizon. The Texas frontier is a rough and difficult environment for young woman even under normal circumstances, and now that we are no longer on peaceful terms with the Mexican government, with Santa Anna threatening to utterly crush all resistance to his tyranny, the situation here is becoming all the more dangerous. Indeed, if matters continue to escalate at the rate they have over the past couple years, I do not see how ultimate conflict is avoidable. " He promised to continue to send her letters regarding his welfare and any new events, and urged her not to try and come to him until it was safe to do so. "I know that this long separation has been hard on you," He added, "And I long for the day when we are reunited to each other, but I am at peace knowing that you are safe and well with Dr. Dopkins. God will see us through this difficult time, my dear little sister, and we must cling to Him, and trust Him with the future."

Mary vividly remembered the growing alarm and dismay she felt upon hearing Ben's tidings, as well as the other disturbing reports that were circulating concerning the troubling state of affairs in Texas. She longed to join her brother and be with him despite any dangers she might face, for up until that time they had always faced their trials and difficulties together.

HE BEGAN TO TAKE HER WITH HIM ON HIS ROUTINE VISITS TO HIS PATIENTS

As the weeks passed, and the prospect of an all-out war between the Texans and the Mexican government grew more and more certain, so also did her intense longing and resolution to join him and support their cause in any way that she could, but how this was to be accomplished, she did not know.

Mary brought to memory the late summer day in 1835 that Dr. Dopkins had discovered her reading a letter that she had just received from Ben. He noticed the troubled look upon her countenance and had inquired as to what caused it. "Oh Sir," she said, "I have just learned of still more disturbing news from my brother. He has written to tell me the Texans have finally determined to break away from Mexico [2], and that he fears the beginning of hostilities is eminent." "Does he plan to take part in the revolt?" Queried Dr. Dopkins. "He does, Sir. He is outraged about the way the Mexican government has been mistreating the Texas settlers and their attempts to strip away their rights, especially as they have done nothing to merit such actions." Mary replied. "I, too, have heard word of these tidings from an old friend of mine," said Dr. Dopkins, "We both served together during the War of 1812, and he just recently relocated to Texas himself, and has done his best to keep me informed on the situation there. Yesterday, I received a letter from him in which he begged me to come and join him, as he believes that there will soon be a great need for the aid I can provide as a former army surgeon." "I did not know that you were an army surgeon, Dr. Dopkins!" Mary exclaimed in surprise. "It is true, my dear." He replied gravely, "The reason I chose the profession I now occupy is because I believed I could best serve my country by attempting to save the lives of her defenders. God knows I attempted to do so with all the strength and skill that I possessed, and it seems as if He is calling me to this purpose yet again." "Have you decided whether you will join your friend in Texas, Sir?" Mary asked eagerly. "Yes, I have, my child. If I can be of any use to the Texas settlers in their struggle for freedom, then it is not only right, but also my duty to join them." "Oh, Doctor Dopkins!" Mary cried, rising hastily to her feet and coming to stand before him, her hands clasped together tightly in her earnestness. "Would you be so good as to allow me to go with you?" "To Texas? At such a time as this? Why girl, you must be mad!" Exclaimed Dr Dopkins in astonishment. "Indeed, I am in earnest, Sir!" Mary answered eagerly. "I had already decided to join Ben after reading his letter, and assist the cause of the Texans in any way possible. The only I difficulty I foresaw was my seeming incapacity to accomplish either purpose, but such a predicament will cease to exist if you will allow me to accompany you." "But my dear child," the doctor began warmly, "I admire your courage, but you must understand that the battlefield is no place for a young woman. Your brother would certainly say as much if he were here, and besides, what help do you imagine you could provide?" "I could go on as you nursing assistant," Mary replied firmly,

"You just mentioned a moment ago yourself that the Texan army will have a tremendous need for medical help once hostilities begin, and with all due respect, Sir, you know as well as I do how much you will need an assistant in your work there!" "But," — Dr Dopkins spluttered, "Well, yes, that is indeed true my dear, but what about your brother? What would he say to all of this?" "Well, Doctor," Mary said quietly, "I admit I don't think that he would be any too eager for my plan, knowing how concerned he is for my safety. However, my determination is set. It is true I cannot endure to be separated from my brother any longer, but more importantly, as you said about yourself, I believe it to be my duty to help the Texans in any way I can, especially since I have the ability to do so. Why Doctor Dopkins, Texas is now the home of both Ben and myself. How could I turn my back on her when she is in such dire distress?"

Mary smiled to herself as she recalled the look on Dr. Dopkin's face as he had finally assented to taking her with him to Texas. After much bustle and preparation, they had started out on their journey at the end of that same month. Their departure was none too soon, for on October 2, 1835, the growing tensions between Mexico and Texas culminated at Gonzales, when the Mexican army arrived to seize control of the Texan's cannon in compliance with Santa Anna's orders to disarm the Mexican citizens and settlers. Instead of surrendering to their demands, a small band of Texans assembled to protect the cannon, resulting in a brief skirmish that sparked the beginning of the Texas war for Independence. After the Battle of Gonzales, the conflict between Mexico and Texas escalated rapidly, as the Texans worked to seize as much ground as possible before the arrival of a larger and more formidable enemy force. They proceeded to seize control of Goliad, securing invaluable munition and supplies in doing so [25], and next turned their attention to the remaining Mexican forces stationed in to San Antonio de Bexar, a vital Mexican stronghold commanded by Mexican General Martin Perfecto de Cos. As the Texans advanced on San Antonio, they engaged the Mexican army in a brief struggle which became known as the *Battle of Concepcion* on October 28, 1835, just outside of the city on the grounds of Concepcion mission [10]. After a heated conflict, they forced the Mexican forces to retreat back to San Antonio, and captured one of their cannons [11]. The Texans then lay siege to the city of San Antonio itself, which ultimately lasted for several long weeks, from October through December. Finally, on December 5, after learning through a Mexican deserter of the weakness of the Mexican position in San Antonio, the Texans began the final attack upon the city itself. After a fierce and bloody four-day battle, and sustaining heavy casualties, General Cos finally surrendered San Antonio to the Texans to the Texans on December 9, and retreated with his army to Mexico. Their defeat and retreat marked a significant victory for the Texans, for it freed Texas, at least temporarily from the military presence of its foes, and left it almost completely in the hands of the Texans [10], [22], [23], [24].

Mary and Dr. Dopkins reached San Antonio just days after the Mexican army had surrendered it to the Texans, and were met with much joy and gratitude by the rag-tag Texan army. Both were soon hard at work, setting up a makeshift hospital and tending to all the wounded men. Meanwhile, the Texans, headed by American military veteran and Texas commander, Sam Houston, began working to strengthen their positions and prepare themselves for the return of the enemy. They set to work at repairing and strengthening the Mexican entrenchments at San Antonio, to prepare for the retaliatory response from Santa Anna and his army that they knew was sure to come. San Antonio de Bexár was considered to be an important fortification, as it was situated on the main roads leading into Texas, thus controlling both supply and communication lines. Such advantages would make it a primary target for Santa Anna, and the Texans were determined to maintain their possession of it, if possible, despite their small numbers and lack of supplies and munitions [11], [22], [24].

Mary sighed as she carefully put the last of the cleaned medical instruments in their case. She and Dr. Dopkins had now been in San Antonio for nearly two weeks, yet all of her attempts to find Ben had come to no avail, and she was growing discouraged. Seven years had passed since

Mary had last seen her brother, and she had not heard a word from him since leaving Tennessee, and thus had little to no knowledge of his recent actions or participation in the Texan revolt. She had learned from some of the men that he had taken part in the siege, but had not been seen or hear of by any of them since its conclusion. This, together with the fruitlessness of her search led her to fear that some ill had befallen him. Could it be, she agonized, that he had been shot down in a skirmish with the enemy or in the siege, or perhaps stricken with some illness, or killed by the marauding Indian tribes?

Mary then thought of what her brother had lovingly instructed her to do whenever she felt anxious or troubled. "Call out to the Lord," He had said, "And He will strengthen you, and give you His perfect peace." Mary knelt down wearily upon the dirt floor of the makeshift hospital, as she had done so many times before, and poured out her heart to her Heavenly Father, asking Him to protect Ben, and lead her to him. She arose again, feeling not a little comforted, knowing that her Lord was with her, and that the same God who loved and cared for her, also loved and was watching over Ben.

Footnotes:

[1] Warren, R. (1958.) *Remember the Alamo!* Random House, Inc.

[2] D'Souza, D. (2014.) *America: Imagine A World Without Her.* Regnery Publishing.

[3] Federer, B. (2022, February 24.) *"Remember the Alamo-Remember Goliad": History of New Spain & Texas Independence-American Minute with Bill Federer.* Retrieved from: https://americanminute.com/blogs/todays-american-minute/remember-the-alamo-remember-goliad-history-of-new-spain-texas-american-minute-with-bill-federer

[10] Minster, Christopher. (2020, August 28). Timeline of the Texas Revolution. Retrieved from: https://www.thoughtco.com/important-dates-in-texas-independence-2136254

[11] TheAlamo.org. (n.d). *Battle and Revolution: Freedoms Worth Fighting For.* Retrieved from: https://www.thealamo.org/remember/battle-and-revolution

[22] Pennybacker, A. (1908) *A History of Texas, Revised.* Mrs. Percy V. Pennybacker Publisher.

[23] Steen, R. (1939) *History of Texas.* The Steck Company Publishers.

[24] Barker, E., & Pohl, J. (2024, March 7). *Texas Revolution*. Retrieved from: https://www.tshaonline.org/handbook/entries/texas-revolution

[25] Hardeman, L. (2020, December 7). *Goliad Campaign of 1835*. Retrieved from: https://texasproud.com/texas-goliad-campaign-of-1835/

[26] TheAlamo.org. (n.d.) *The Importance of Béxar and the Alamo in the Texas Revolution*. Retrieved from: https://www.thealamo.org/remember/battle-and-revolution/bexar

[27] Captivating History. (2020) *History of Texas*. Captivating History

Chapter 2

The Reunion

"Well, Mary, my dear," Dr. Dopkins said a few days after the opening of this story, as he and Mary partook of their simple breakfast fare together, "I'm afraid that the time is drawing near for us to move on from this place." "Why is that Dr. Dopkins?" Mary asked, trying to hide the displeasure that this unwelcome statement had brought her. Dr. Dopkins reached across the table to put a fatherly hand on her arm, for he fully realized how she was longing to find her brother, and that the thought that she might fail to complete her search for him in that area — thus leaving room for the possibility that she might miss him — was anything but pleasing to her. "Unfortunately, my child," he replied, "Our work here will come to an end before much longer, as most of the wounded are convalescing rapidly, and will soon cease to require any medical care. Many of the volunteers are returning to their homes while the temporary cessation of hostilities lasts, while others, though fewer in number, are traveling to join Sam Houston, who is working to build up a regular army [1] in preparation for the return of the enemy forces. I believe it would be wise for us to depart as soon as we are no longer of any use here, and to join Sam Houston to offer our services to him. Surely you would agree that this is the most prudent path for us to take?" "Indeed I do, Sir." Mary answered, sighing as she did so. "I know how greatly you desire to find your brother Ben, my dear," the doctor continued kindly, "But have you not considered the possibility of his already being with Houston, or that perhaps he is planning to join him also?" "I hadn't thought of that," Mary said more hopefully, her countenance brightening as she did so, "It is only the thought of my missing him here that troubles me. But surely that is not possible after all this time, particularly as the number of Texans remaining here has been steadily diminishing by the day!" "Very true, my child," Dr Dopkins replied, "Are you in agreement with me then, concerning our departure?" "Yes Sir, I am." Mary said, forcing herself to smile, for notwithstanding everything the good doctor had said to comfort her, she could not suppress the uneasiness she felt about leaving San Antonio so soon. However, she also had no desire to inconvenience Dr. Dopkins, especially after all of his kindness to her, and neither did she wish to lose sight of the main reason for their coming to Texas.

After the morning meal was over, Dr. Dopkins and Mary set off on their routine visit to their patients, and after he had completed his tasks, the Doctor left Mary to her work, and begin making the arrangements for their departure.

"Colonel Neill, your scout, Drury, has just returned from his inspection of the Alamo, and is waiting to give you his report." "Thank you, Sergeant Davis. Please show him in." Replied Colonel Neill. The Colonel had been left in command of San Antonio de Bexar after the siege, and he had recently been in communication with Houston concerning their situation, which unfortunately, was anything but satisfactory. His small garrison of about 100 men was entirely insufficient to withstand any significant attack [4], and to make matters still worse, most of the men were poorly clad and payed, and many were threatening to return to their homes. To top it off, Colonel Neill could not even acquire horses for necessary scouting purposes, which left him almost completely in the dark regarding the advance of the enemy. Consequently, there was grave doubt the Texans could hold their position, notwithstanding the fact that both Bexar and its sister city, Goliad, would make a very good line of defense against the enemy [1].

Despite the odds, Colonel Neill had no desire to abandon his position at Bexar [1], and had that morning sent one of his most trusted scouts, a volunteer from Tennessee named Ben Drury, to inspect an old abandoned mission that was referred to by the Mexican inhabitants of Bexar as, "The Alamo". The Colonel hoped that if necessary, the Alamo would serve as a reliable fortress should the expected arrival of Santa Anna and his army force them to pull back from the town of San Antonio itself.

"Private Drury, Sir." Stated Sergeant Davis, as he ushered the aforementioned scout into his commander's humble quarters. "Well Drury, what news do you — good heavens, man! Whatever has happened to you?" Was the somewhat startled exclamation the Colonel uttered as he caught sight of Ben Drury's pale and haggard face, and upon closer inspection of his person, he noticed that his right arm was done up in a makeshift sling. "Oh, nothing much, Sir," Ben replied with a weak laugh, "I am only the unlucky victim of a most peculiar accident. While I was inspecting the old chapel inside the Alamo, one of the young volunteers who was with me took it into his head to test the strength of the decrepit support beams. In doing so, the fellow dislodged a particularly large old beam, which I unfortunately happened to be in the path of. It gave my shoulder a rather unfriendly rap, but thankfully not much damage appears to be done." "I don't think that your injuries are as minor as you make them out to be Drury," Colonel Neill replied, "And I insist that you pay a visit to the doctor as soon as you have finished giving me your report. You had better take a seat before you begin though, for you don't appear to be at all steady on your feet." "Thank you, Sir," Ben said, sinking wearily into a chair as instructed, "I guess that beam must have knocked my head a bit as it struck my shoulder. But might I ask how there came to be a doctor here? I have been away on

33

scouting missions so often during the past few weeks that I'm afraid I'm quite ignorant regarding any new happenings here." "He and his assistant arrived several weeks ago from Tennessee, and have rendered us great service by attending to our wounded." The Colonel answered, "Heaven knows how much we needed them, seeing as we are depleted of both medical supplies and physicians." Colonel Neil paused for a moment after he uttered these last words, as the gravity of their situation was recalled to his mind once again.

"Now Drury," He went on at last, "What do you have to report concerning the state of the Alamo?" "Not the best news Sir," Ben began, "It's a rather ancient mission, and though it must have been quite grand at one time, it is now very run down, and parts of the walls appeared to be quite dilapidated and in need of much repair. The same could be said of the chapel and barracks inside its walls, although certain parts of the latter are better preserved than others. Inside of the Alamo, there is a large area that appears to be a sort of courtyard, with rows of old barracks lining its sides. To the east of the courtyard lies a fair sized cattle pen that is surrounded by a worn down picket fence. There is also another small area that is attached to the south side of cattle pen, as well as an old chapel [1]." "Do you think there is any possibility of the Alamo being used as a place of defense, Drury?" Asked the Colonel somewhat anxiously, "Well, Sir," Ben said thoughtfully, "All of the buildings desperately need repair work, and it will take some time for us to get it into something like fighting shape, but I think that the old mission will do alright in a pinch for our fall-back position." Colonel Neill then went on to ask Ben more specific questions about the Alamo, and the outbuildings and terrain that surrounded it. At the conclusion of their interview, he said warmly, "Drury, the services you have rendered me during your time here have been indispensable, and the information you have just related has helped me to answer a question that I have been seriously pondering for some time of late. I now have pressing business to attend to, but I will send for you again this evening to discuss your next assignment." "Thank you, Sir." Ben answered gratefully, as he rose to make his departure. However, he was forced to catch hold of his chair for support due to a sudden feeling of faintness, which Colonel Neill did not fail to observe. "I will have Davis escort you to the Doctor." He said firmly, and despite Ben's protestations, the aforementioned sergeant was sent for. Upon his arrival, he proceeded to lead Ben to the makeshift hospital, often lending him his support along the way, as Ben's head was giving him more trouble than he cared to admit.

"I do not understand how I could get through the siege of San Antonio unscathed, only to be banged up by a chance falling beam!" Ben exclaimed with a hint of frustration in his tone as they neared the hospital. "Take it easy, Drury!" Exclaimed Davis with a grin. "I'd be grateful that your injuries aren't any worse than they are. Just think of what a fix you'd be in if the full weight of that beam came crashing down on your head instead of just glancing it — why man, it could have crushed your skull!" "Oh, it's not that I'm ungrateful Davis, it's just that I'm not looking forward to seeing that doctor very much. Doctors always come up with the most absurd and impossible notions of keeping a fellow in bed for a minor head cold, or some other trifling affair — you know how it is! I hate to think what he might prescribe for my case."

By this time, the two men had reached their destination, and Davis made his comrade sit in a chair just inside the doorway while he went to find the doctor. Ben leaned his aching head in his hand and listened half interestedly to Davis as he inquired of one of the wounded men as to where the doctor might be found. He was much chagrined when he heard the fellow answer that the doctor was out just then, and that his assistant alone was caring for the wounded in his absence. "Confound it!" Ben thought wearily to himself, "The assistant is bound to be worse than the doctor — probably will try to prove his skill by prescribing some outrageous treatment!" He settled back in his chair with a sigh to await his companion's return. It wasn't long before he heard him returning, and glancing up listlessly, he observed him approaching with a young woman at his side. "He's right over here Ma'am," He heard Davis say, "Thank you kindly for coming to look at him." "Oh, it's no trouble at all!" She replied, "I won't be able to help him as much as the doctor will when he returns, but I will do all I can in the meantime. Might I ask how your friend received his injury?" "It was a rather strange accident Ma'am, you see he was struck by a" — And here, Davis broke off his sentence in astonishment. As soon as Ben heard Mary's voice, he started violently, jerked himself bolt upright, and gazed hard at her. Once he was able to get a good look at her face, there was no doubt in his mind as to who she was. He lurched to his feet so suddenly that he toppled over his chair, and, taking one faltering step forward, exclaimed, "Mary! Is it possible, or did I hit my head harder than I imagined?" Mary gave a little cry of joy, and in the next instant she was in her brother's arms, sobbing, "Ben, oh Ben! God has answered my prayers, and I have found you!"

For a little while, the two reunited siblings were oblivious to everything going on around them. As soon as he had recovered from his surprise, Sergeant Davis smiled and quietly exited the scene, clapping Ben on the back in congratulation as he passed. This brought Mary back to her senses again, and she gave a little laugh and carefully extracted herself from Ben's embrace. "Goodness," she cried, "I must not neglect my duty! Come with me to the back room, Ben, so that I can have a look at that shoulder and we can talk in private." "Oh, hang my shoulder!" Ben answered with a grin. "I've forgotten all about it since seeing you, and besides, I hardly even feel the pain anymore." "Still, I must attend to it, Ben," Mary insisted, tugging gently at his uninjured arm, "Else you will not be fit for your duties. While I work we can talk together, for we have seven long years' worth of time to get caught up on!" Ben then allowed himself to be led along to the back room Mary had spoken of, and before long, the two of them were both eagerly talking away as she examined his shoulder.

As she worked, Ben related to Mary how he had been obliged to abandon his efforts on their homestead to join the Texan army soon after the Battle of Gonzales. Thanks to his familiarity with San Antonio and the surrounding countryside, he had gone on to serve in the capacity of a scout during the siege and attack upon the city. After the conclusion of the siege, he was sent on a secret and highly extensive scouting mission to track the enemy retreat from San Antonio and watch for the return of the enemy forces, and had only recently returned to the city to help assess the Texan defenses. Because of the nature of his missions, he had not returned to the city since the conclusion of the siege, and had been in very little contact with the Texan army, which is why Mary had been unable to learn of his whereabouts. Ben also informed Mary of how, after the siege, he had traveled back to their homestead to retrieve some supplies, only to discover that it had been utterly ravaged and destroyed by the retreating Mexican army. This sad discovery had left him in turmoil, for he realized that he no longer had any home for Mary to come to, and that unless the Texans were able to achieve total victory and independence from Mexico, all that they had worked and prayed for would be in vain. "That is why I know I must stay in this fight to the end, Mary," He concluded, "Otherwise there will be no future here for us or our children, and nothing will be left for us but an unthinkable existence under tyranny." "I quite agree with you, Ben." Mary answered quietly, "And that is why I have come to join you." She then proceeded to tell Ben of how she and Dr. Dopkins had traveled to Texas to support the Texan's cause, and of their work to care for the wounded from the siege of San Antonio, and their plans to continue their efforts throughout the duration of the conflict.

After Ben had heard Mary's story, he leaned back in his chair and drew a deep breath. "Well Mary," He said at last, "I really shouldn't be so overjoyed to have you here, seeing as how dangerous and uncertain the current situation is, and I half wish that you had remained in Tennessee where you would have been safe. But I'm also awfully glad to see you again. I never imagined that I would be gone for so long, or that circumstances here would take such a hostile turn. There were several occasions when I wondered if I'd ever see you again... and that was a hard possibility to face, I can tell you. Though I am sorry to have you in such a dangerous environment, I also cannot thank God enough for bringing you safely here to me, and that we are back together again." "So am I, Ben," Mary answered, giving his hand a gentle squeeze. "And I must add that I am grateful that you injured your shoulder as you did — not that I'm happy you were hurt, of course, but your injury was the means which God used to reunite us. Dr. Dopkins and I were planning to leave Bexar to join Sam Houston within a couple days, and if you had not been forced to come to me, I probably would have missed you, and who knows if we would have seen each other again after that?" Ben looked at Mary in astonishment as she uttered these last words. "Indeed!" He exclaimed, "Now I could kick myself for all the fuss I made about the inconvenience I thought my accident caused me! I hope I never complain about anything of the sort again, for one never knows what God has in store when He allows such events to occur." Mary laughed merrily at this statement, "Thankfully," she said, "Your injuries are not too severe, and from what I can tell, it appear that you only have a minor fracture, although Dr. Dopkins will inform you better when he has a chance to examine you."

"Do you not still plan to leave with the doctor Mary?" Ben queried, "You would probably be much safer with him than you would be with me." "No, Ben." Mary replied in a gentle, but earnest tone, "My place is with you, and wherever you go, I will go. When we last parted, I vowed that if God allowed us to be reunited, I would never permit myself to be separated from you again, and as far as I am concerned, nothing but death itself shall separate us from each other." Ben put his arm around Mary and drew her closer to him, his heart too full for words. She, in return, also passed her small arm around him, and leaned her head on his shoulder. "Whatever happens," she said softly,

"And whatever the end of this struggle might be, the only thing that matters is that we will have done our duty to both God and man... and that we will be together."

Footnotes:

[1] Warren, R. (1958.) *Remember the Alamo!* Random House, Inc.

Chapter 3

The Alamo

When Dr. Dopkins returned, he was both astonished and overjoyed to learn of Mary's reunion with Ben. He had made arrangements for both he and Mary to join Sam Houston and his army, planning that they should leave within two days' time with a small detachment of Texans, who were traveling there as well. He was not the least bit surprised, however, when he heard of Mary's decision to remain with her brother, and did not make any attempt to dissuade her, though he knew he would feel the loss of her presence sorely. Not only had her assistance proved to be invaluable to him, but he had also come to care for her as if she were his own daughter.

Later that same evening, Colonel Neill sent for Ben. He ordered him to oversee the rough repair of the Alamo, and placed a small group of Texan volunteers for that purpose at his disposal. He also informed Ben that he had received word from Houston that Jim Bowie was on his way to the Alamo with thirty men [1]. "Have you decided to remain in Bexar then, Sir?" Ben queried, "Well Drury, I believe I will wait and consult with Bowie before I make my final decision. However, unless he can convince me otherwise, after hearing your report this afternoon, I have resolved to hold fast here." "I am glad to hear that, Sir." Ben replied, "I should be very sorry to leave San Antonio for our foes to repossess after all the work it took for us to drive them out of it." "I feel the same way, Drury," answered the Colonel, "And I am certain that Houston would as well if it weren't for the fact that we are cripplingly short of both men and supplies. Consequentially, in our current state, there is no certainty that we can maintain our position." "I understand, Sir." Ben replied gravely. "I heard from Davis about your discovery of your sister." Colonel Neill went on again, more lightly. "Yes Sir," Ben said, "She is actually the assistant of the doctor who arrived recently." "Truly?" The Colonel exclaimed, somewhat incredulously, "Does she plan to remain with you, then? I understand that the good doctor is leaving here shortly." "Yes Sir, she does." Ben answered, "I'm afraid no amount of talking will convince her to leave me, no matter how dangerous the situation here might become." "She sounds like quite a girl!" laughed the Colonel. "Indeed, she is, Sir!" Ben replied with a grin, "And I am proud to claim her as my sister."

The day of Dr. Dopkins' departure arrived all too soon for that kind gentleman and Mary. "Well, my dear," he said, when the time came for him to bid her farewell, "I shall miss both your help and your presence, but I know I am leaving you happy, and in good hands." "Oh yes, Doctor," Mary replied, "And I will do my best to continue on with the work here in your absence." "I know you will my child," The doctor replied kindly, "And I cannot express how greatly I appreciate all of your assistance. You have been a treasure to me, Mary, and I don't know how I am going to manage without you." "Thank you, Sir," Mary replied, her eyes filling with tears as she spoke, "I don't know what I would have done without you when Ben was away, and can't ever thank you enough for everything that you have done for me." "Yes indeed, Doctor," Ben interjected warmly, "It gave me such peace of mind to know that my sister was with you, and I don't know how I will ever be able to repay you for all the kindness that you showed her."

"No thanks are needed, my children," Dr. Dopkins replied. "I am proud to know two such remarkable young people, and any help that I was able to offer you has been a pleasure. Please God, our parting will not be a long one, and we will see each other again under happier circumstances." He then shook hands with Ben, gave Mary a fatherly embrace, and then turned to climb into the wagon that was to carry him to his destination. As he and his party departed, Dr. Dopkins turned to look back at Mary and Ben, who were standing side by side, and said to himself, "May God bless and protect those dear children, for they almost certainly will face hard times before much longer."

For the first couple weeks after Dr. Dopkin's departure, life remained somewhat uneventful for the Drury siblings. They both lodged in the same quarters that Mary and Dr. Dopkins had shared previously, and every day Ben would head off to the Alamo with his men to oversee necessary repairs, which he took an active part in as soon as his rapidly mending shoulder would allow. While he was away, Mary busied herself with attending to the remaining wounded men who still needed medical care, as well as helping the other women with washing, mending, and cooking for the rest of the detachment.

Ben and Mary treasured every free moment they spent together, and during these rare times, they would often go on long walks through the surrounding countryside or through the bustling city of San Antonio, admiring the beauty of the Spanish architecture and perusing the Mexican wares sold in the vibrant market square. Sometimes, Ben would take Mary with him to the Alamo and show her the progress that was being made there, and these were excursions that always brought her great pleasure. There were also times when the two of them were too tired to do much, and when this was the case, they would simply sit and indulge in long conversations, and the enjoyment of each other's company. Most often, their conversations would turn to their homestead and future plans. Ben often described their homestead site to Mary, and promised to take her to visit it as soon as it was safe to do so. They both loved to discuss their plans for rebuilding their homestead, and talk of the cattle operation they hoped to someday own, and the families they would raise together. "It is almost hard to imagine such good times are possible when we are in the midst of so much conflict and uncertainty." Mary said pensively one evening during such a conversation, as she and Ben sat together on the steps of their small adobe hut, watching the sunset. "I know what you mean." Ben replied, leaning his head back to rest against the adobe wall. "But if you think of it, it is almost always hardest to remember the light and brilliance of the sun when you are in the middle of a severe storm. Sometimes, it can even seem like that storm will never cease, but in the end, it will always pass over, and the sun will shine once again, perhaps even brighter than before." Ben turned from his musings to look at his sister. "This conflict will end Mary," he said quietly, "And God-willing, when it is truly over, we will be blessed with the knowledge that our children will live a life of freedom." "What a blessed day that will be." Mary murmured, gazing off into the western skies at the beautiful gold and pink sunset hues. "Indeed it will be," Ben answered, his eyes returning to the sky, "And ultimately, it is for that day that we are fighting for. Always remember that, Sis."

The arrival of the famous knife-wielding, Indian fighter Jim Bowie and his men caused quite the stir amongst the small detachment in Bexar, especially as it soon began to be rumored that they had been sent to help destroy the Alamo, and pull back with any cannons and supplies to the north of San Antonio. However, Ben soon learned from Colonel Neill that Bowie had firmly agreed with his plan to hold the Alamo at all costs rather than abandon it to the enemy. Additionally, they were soon joined by a certain Lieutenant Colonel Travis who had also been ordered to the Alamo, along with the thirty men who accompanied him [1].

Many of the Texans were, though true patriots at heart, of a rather wild sort. Many of the regulars and volunteers stoutly refused to take part in any drills or fortification repairs, and instead preferred to preoccupy themselves with carousing, rough sports, and the remaining attractions that San Antonio held [1]. Despite this, Ben continued on doggedly with his work, and Mary did her best to adjust and accustom herself to the habits of rugged individuals who pervaded the area.

To her surprise and pleasure, Mary soon discovered a new friend in the person of a young woman her age named Susanna Dickinson, the young wife of Lieutenant Dickinson. Mary was extremely grateful for this God-sent friendship, for it soon brought much brightness and encouragement to her toil-filled days, and the two young women spent many hours of each day together, attending to the various domestic tasks that necessity required of them.

Mary was also pleased to make the acquaintance of John Sutherland, a physician who had come to join the Texans in Bexar [1]. After their meeting, she had resolved to turn over the charge of the patients under her care to him, and then work to assist him as she had Dr. Dopkins. However, after Dr. Sutherland assessed the welfare of the patients as she requested, he reported the wounded men were thriving under her care, and insisted that it was not at all necessary for any changes to be made. "I am quite unused to seeing women involved in this sort of work," he had said, "Particularly such as young as yourself. You are doing an admirable work here, Miss Drury, and please know that I will always be willing and ready to assist you whenever you require my services." Ben felt ready to burst with pride when he heard these praises of his sister and never failed to encourage and acclaim her. She was not alone in receiving approbation, for Jim Bowie himself had not failed to notice Ben and his men at their work. They had greatly improved the condition of the Alamo by patching up its walls in several places, setting up some fresh bulwarks, as well as adding scaffolding for the Texans to mount for the defense of the walls. Bowie had warmly commended Ben on his progress, and never failed to encourage him in the continuance of his task. "For as old and decrepit as that old mission might be," he told Ben, "It might soon become our stronghold and place of refuge, should the Mexican forces dare to advance upon us."

Late one afternoon, Ben came hurrying back from his work to the small adobe hut that he and Mary were lodged in, much earlier than was his wont. "Mary! Good gracious Mary, where are you?" He cried eagerly as he burst through the door. "Good gracious yourself Ben, I'm here," she replied with a laugh. "I was just trying to mend these torn breeches of yours. Is anything the matter? I thought you would be at your work for some time longer, as usual. Is it dinnertime already, and I missed the time?" "Well, it is almost time for dinner to be sure," Ben answered, coming to stand beside her, a tremendous grin upon his face, "However, that is not why I've returned early. I couldn't get any more work out of the men today, as the arrival of a very important individual interrupted us." "Really?" Mary asked, looking up from her work, "Who is it?" "You probably won't believe me when I tell you, Mary," Ben said, struggling to suppress his excitement, "But another group of men have just arrived from Tennessee, and they were led by none other than Davy Crockett himself!" "Truly!" Mary exclaimed in astonishment, leaping to her feet, and dropping her work as she did so. "It is just as true as I am standing here before you, Sis!" Ben replied joyfully, and filled with mirth at Mary's astounded expression, mischievously swept his little sister up in his strong arms and spun with her around the room.

"Ben — Ben, you must stop!" Mary cried laughingly after a couple of turns. "You are making my head spin even worse than it already is! Oh, but I can't hardly believe it! Colonel Crockett here, in Bexar!" "I know Mary, I still haven't quite got over the shock myself." Ben answered, gently setting her down again, his face aglow with excitement. "To think that after all the tales we heard of him in Tennessee, we should finally get to meet him under these circumstances!" "It's almost unbelievable!" Mary exclaimed, "He was our childhood hero —" "And still is, I might add!" "Why, of course he still is Ben, but as I was saying, it's just so hard to believe that he has actually come here! Do you really think we might get a chance to meet him?" "I'm certain of it." Ben said, "Speaking of which, let's go and see if we can do so right now! Last I heard, he went to speak with the commanding officers, but I'm sure that his interview with them must be over by this time." As Ben uttered these last words, he tucked Mary's hand under his arm, and started for the door with such speed that she scarcely had time to seize her hat on the way out.

They soon arrived at Colonel Neill's quarters, before which quite a crowd of men had already gathered, and were just in time to see a very tall individual in buckskins and wearing a coonskin cap emerge from the doorway. The men all gave a cheer when they saw him, which he answered by raising his hand in a friendly salute, shouting as he did so, "Thank you boys, it certainly is an honor to be here with you. I hope that my comrades and I will help you strike such a blow for freedom as that great despot Santa Anna can never recover from!" At this, the men uttered a terrific roar, and some of them even threw their hats into the air and whooped with enthusiasm. Before long, the great man was mingling with the men, shaking hands and exchanging remarks with them.

Mary clung tightly to Ben's arm as they stood at the outskirts of the crowd. "We'll wait here, Sis," He said, "There's no use in you getting shoved about in the crowd. Colonel Crockett is bound to pass us as he leaves the commander's quarters, and perhaps we will get a chance to speak to him then." They hadn't long to wait, as before much more time had passed, Davy Crockett finally managed to break away from the enthusiastic crowd crying, "Alright now boys, I must go and see to it that both my comrades and our steeds get situated in their respective quarters, but be assured that I will be a'joining you again shortly so that we may become better acquainted." He was just about to proceed on his way when Ben stepped up to him, with Mary at his side. "Before you go Sir," He said, removing his hat as he spoke, "My sister and I wish to thank you for coming to join in our cause for the freedom of Texas. We both have the utmost respect for you, Sir, and it will be both an honor and a privilege to fight alongside you." "Thanks, Son," Crockett answered kindly, "An' might I inquire as to whom

I have the pleasure of speakin' to?" "I'm Ben Drury Sir, and this is my sister Mary." "I am pleased to meet you Drury, and you too, Miss," turning to Mary and doffing his cap to her. "I must say," He continued, "It does a body good to see such young folks as yourselves so engaged in this struggle for liberty. Tell me, are the two of you native to these parts, or are you settlers?" "We are settlers, Sir," Ben replied. "As a matter of fact, we are both originally from Tennessee." "Is that so? Well then, I am all the more glad to make your acquaintance, and as soon as my comrades and I are settled an' all, I would be pleased to talk more with you." "Thank you, Colonel Crockett!" Mary said, beaming, "It would be an honor, Sir!" Came from Ben, warmly, and the two of them stepped aside to let him pass. "Oh, and one more thing," He called over his shoulder as he continued on his way, "Let's hear no more of this 'Sir' nonsense! It's just plain Davy Crockett — remember, we're all equals in this fight!"

Footnotes:

[1] Warren, R. (1958.) *Remember the Alamo!* Random House, Inc.

Chapter 4

The Arrival of the Enemy

For the next couple of days, the Texans spent most of their time with Davy Crockett. He thoroughly enjoyed their company, and it wasn't long before he had them all laughing and joking over the 'tall tales' which he was so fond of relating, and though some of them were rather outrageous, they did much to lighten the previously tense atmosphere. Somehow, Ben managed to keep up with his work at repairing the Alamo, and continued to make such steady progress that even Davy Crockett seemed to take quite an interest in it. The latter would often come out to the Alamo to note any new progress Ben and his men were making, stating that he would like to be well acquainted with the place he might soon be "holed up" in. He also visited the recuperating wounded men under Mary's care and was well pleased to witness Mary's skill and devotion to them. His presence brought much satisfaction and delight to her patients, and helped them not to feel their temporary confinement as keenly. The more time Crockett spent with the Drury siblings, the fonder he became of them, and it wasn't long before they both looked upon him as a father figure rather than a distant legend.

As the somewhat redundant days wore on, Davy Crockett continued to do what he could to provide cheer and good humor for the Texans. He seemed to be almost constantly either telling of his hunting expeditions or exchanging humorous jokes with the men, and occasionally, he even entertained them with his fiddle (which, not being one of his strong points, was more of a source of amusement than anything). More often than not, the married men would take these opportunities to dance with their wives, an event that Ben and Mary never failed to take part in. It was always a happy sight to see them whirling too and fro, in and out amongst the other dancers, their eyes shining, and their faces beaming with mirth and pleasure.

IT WAS A HAPPY SIGHT TO SEE THEM WHIRLING IN AND OUT AMONGST THE OTHER DANCERS

Despite all these attempts to ease the tension, many of the men struggled to maintain discipline, becoming uneasy and restless from the protracted suspense caused by the delay in the expected enemy forces [1]. Unexpectedly, Colonel Neill was forced to make his departure upon receiving word that his family had been struck with serious illness, and as a result, he turned over command of the Texas regulars to Travis [4]. Jim Bowie, however, retained command of the volunteers, who far outnumbered the regulars who were under Travis. Consequently, the two men were constantly striving against each other, both desiring to have the position of absolute authority over the defenders. After many a fiery dispute, they finally agreed to take joint command [1], a decision which helped to restore some of the order that had been lost after Colonel Neill's departure.

As the dust from the heated change in command settled, time continued to drag by all the more slowly for the Texan detachment. Rumors began to circulate in Bexar concerning a great enemy force under the command of General Santa Anna that was headed in their direction. Though the rest of the men largely disregarded these rumors, Ben did not dismiss them, and began to seriously consider the chances of their small force withstanding a full-scale assault. He became increasingly uneasy about Mary's safety, and often questioned whether he had been wise in allowing her to remain with him. Though he never voiced his concerns to her, Ben noticed an abnormal gravity and thoughtfulness in Mary that he was unaccustomed to seeing. After some time, he inquired if anything was troubling her, but she always smiled in response and made some light excuse. The truth was that Mary, too, had not failed to note the rumored advance of the Mexican forces, and though she did not share any of her fears with Ben, she too often wondered about what might happen if they were to attack. These thoughts sometimes filled her with a heavy feeling that was almost akin to dread, just as if some great storm was gathering over them, ready to burst.

With every new day, more and more reports of the approaching Mexican army were relayed back to the small band of Texans, which they continued to stoutly disregard, stating that they were probably lies that were intended to drive them from their post. However, these reports were not ignored by the inhabitants of San Antonio de Bexar, who soon packed up their possessions and made their flight with all possible haste. This occurrence became so marked, that it was finally observed by the Texans by the late date of February 23. Despite even these telling signs, they still refused to pay heed to any of the reports or rumors, and no changes were made to the daily routine, except that Travis stationed a man on the roof of the old church as a watch, with orders to ring the bell if he sighted the enemy [1].

The time for this alarm came sooner than expected, as later that same day, the loud pealing of the church bell aroused the Texans. Startled, they quickly thronged before the church to hear the news. "What is it, man?" Travis shouted to the watchman as soon as he had descended from the roof. "I saw them Colonel Travis, Sir! I saw them!" The man replied, breathless with his efforts and excitement, "They are headed straight toward us, and it looks to be a pretty large force!" "Oh, you're just see'in things!" One volunteer exclaimed, having scrambled up to the roof to see what he could for himself, "I see nothing but open spaces and brush!" "I tell you, I did see them!" The watchman shouted back angrily, "The brush may have hidden them, but they are there alright!" "Aw, you've been in the sun too long!" "Yes, why don't you go somewhere and cool off so you can see straight?" Were some of the remarks hurled back at the agitated man. "Oh come, come now!" Exclaimed Doctor Sutherland, pushing his way through the crowd, "Instead of standing around here all day, arguing, I suggest we send out a couple men to investigate this sighting, for if there happens to be any truth in it, we certainly would not want to be caught off guard. I will go myself, but would be much obliged if someone here who knows the country would come along with me." "I'll go with you, Sir, if Colonel Travis is willing!" Cried Ben from the crowd, eagerly surging forward to come and stand by the doctor's side. "And I!" called another individual by the name of John Smith, who also shouldered his way through the throng to join the two men.

"Dr. Sutherland, gentlemen, I sincerely appreciate your willingness to go on this errand," Colonel Travis said warmly, "And I heartily accept your proposal. I will have some of the men saddle up mounts for you and bring them around to the main gate. I know I need not add that you will have to exercise extreme caution on this mission, for if the report from the watchman is indeed true, you may very well have a hot time of it trying to return." "We will be careful, Sir." Ben replied, his two companions nodding in agreement. As the three men proceeded to their quarters to prepare for their scouting mission, Travis walked over to Ben. "I thank you for volunteering your services, Drury," He said, "You are the best scout in this detachment, and I know I can count on you to make an honest report." "Indeed you can, Sir, thank you!" Ben answered, trying his best to hide his pleasure, and giving Travis a hasty salute before hurrying on his way.

In almost less time than it takes to tell, the three men were ready to make their departure. Just before Ben climbed into the saddle of his horse, Mary hastened forward to his side. "Ben," she said, laying her hand on his arm and looking up into his face, striving to hide her worry as she did so, "I will pray for you every minute until you return, and I know God will watch over you. Do be careful though, won't you?" "I will, Sis, don't you worry!" Ben replied, giving her a quick hug, and then turning back again to mount his steed.

The three men rode out of the gate, and on towards the direction in which the enemy had last been reported to be seen, while the watchman quickly took his place once more upon the roof of the old chapel to note their progress. The signal that the three scouts had arranged with him was namely that if they were to return at a normal pace, all was well, but if they were to be seen racing back again, he would know that they had observed the enemy's approach [1]. Upon learning that he was the most familiar with the surrounding country, Doctor Sutherland had ordered Ben to lead their small party, and the latter kept them going on at a brisk pace, though he made certain that they took the advantage of every bit of cover they came upon. They had only gone about a mile and a half from Bexar [1] when Ben suddenly drew in his horse and signaled for his companions to do the same. "What is it Drury?" Queried the Doctor, "Please, Sir, not so loud!" Answered Ben in a whisper, "I could have sworn that I heard something up yonder — almost sounded like metal on metal, or something of that nature. I think I had better go on that ridge just ahead on my own to see what it was about." "Very well, Drury, we will wait for you here." Doctor Sutherland replied, as Ben passed the reins of his horse to him, and slipped quietly from his saddle. He then proceeded to make his way carefully to the aforementioned ridge, stopping often along the way to listen. When he finally reached the knoll, his two comrades watched as he slowly crawled to its top and peered cautiously over. Both men felt their hearts quicken when they saw Ben quickly steal down from the knoll again, and hurry back towards them as rapidly as he could. "It's them!" He exclaimed, in a low, agitated voice, as soon as he got close enough, "It's the Mexican calvary! And not only are there hundreds upon hundreds of them, but they are dangerously close, and we must make haste if we are to get back to Bexar ahead of them!" So saying, Ben sprang into the saddle of his horse, and the three companions began the journey back to the Texan stronghold, urging their horses into full gallop, and each praying silently that they might arrive in safety to warn their comrades of the impending danger.

They made good time, and were three quarters of the way to their destination before they could see the approaching Mexican calvary, which, for the time being, showed no sign of observing their presence. Suddenly, Dr. Sutherland's horse slipped on a muddy slope, throwing its rider violently to the ground before it, too, crashed down across the doctor's legs [1]. Ben turned back hastily upon witnessing the accident of his comrade. "Hurry on to Bexar, Smith, and warn the men!" He cried, "I'll fetch the Doctor!" He was soon at the good man's side, and quickly dragged him away from the struggling beast. "Are you much hurt, Sir?" He exclaimed anxiously. "I don't think so," answered the Doctor in a rather shaky voice. "It's just that my legs don't seem able to hold me." "Not to worry, Sir, I'll help you get mounted again." Ben said, quickly going to the doctor's horse, which had now scrambled to its feet. After leading it back to its rider, he helped Dr. Sutherland to get remounted, and the two of them were soon seen continuing on their interrupted journey at a breakneck speed.

By the time they rode into Bexar, all was in an uproar, as Travis had given the order for all the defenders and non-combatants to pull back to the Alamo. The two men hurried to the Colonel to give their report. "How many calvary would you estimate there were, Drury?" He asked Ben when he had heard their story. "I would say well over a thousand, Sir, and all well mounted." Ben replied. Travis looked grave. "Indeed," he answered in a low voice, "Then there must be thousands more not far behind. Doctor Sutherland," turning to the Doctor, who was still being supported by Ben, "Do you think you are well enough to ride to Gonzales and see if you can get any men there to come to our aid? I will also send a messenger to Goliad for the same purpose, for if we are to hold our position here we desperately need reinforcements, and — well, Doctor, I don't think that those legs of yours will do you good service when the fighting starts." "I am certainly well enough to deliver the message, Sir," the good doctor replied, "And I will take my departure immediately." "Thank you Doctor Sutherland, I wish you Godspeed!" Exclaimed Travis, ringing Sutherland's hand heartily. The doctor was once again assisted onto his horse, and after a final wave, he wielded his steed about again and rode off towards Gonzales.

"Do you know where my sister Mary is, Sir?" Ben asked Travis after the doctor had departed. "Yes, Drury, I saw to it that she was escorted with the other women to the Alamo, and," He added with a smile, "Last I heard, she was busily preoccupied with setting up a hospital in the old chapel." "The dear girl!" Ben exclaimed. "How I wish she were far away from this place in safety!" Travis only sighed heavily in response to this statement. "Do you think we can hold out, Sir?" Ben asked quietly, facing the Colonel squarely, and looking searchingly into his face, "I don't know Drury," He answered, turning to gaze off toward the approaching enemy forces. "If help arrives in time from Goliad and Gonzales, I'm certain we can hold this old mission until the enemy is starved into defeat. Regardless of what might occur, however," He now turned back to face Ben again, "We must hold out here as long as possible to buy Houston time to rally our comrades, and build an army large enough to deal the death blow to our despotic foes. Strange as it may seem, our stand here may decide the fate of the cause of freedom for all of Texas... and whether our children will live a life of freedom, or of servitude. We must never forget what we are fighting for, Drury, and why we must never surrender or retreat, regardless of what the cost might be."

Footnotes:

[1] Warren, R. (1958.) *Remember the Alamo!* Random House, Inc.

[4] Giorello, J. (2016.) *Bunker Hill to WWI: Great Battles for Boys.* Rolling Wheel Publishing.

Chapter 5

Will Help Come?

The news of the approach of Santa Anna's army thoroughly aroused the Texans from their previous apathy. Fully conscious of their impending danger, they swiftly evacuated all of their women and children from San Antonio de Bexar and brought them to the safety of old fort's sheltering walls, after which they returned to the town to gather necessary supplies and provisions to sustain them through the siege. Providentially, they discovered a substantial supply of corn in some of the town's abandoned houses and even rounded up a large herd of cattle, which they promptly drove into the Alamo's stock pens. These desperately needed provisions were received with much gratitude, and would more than amply replenish their depleted supplies to sustain them through a protracted enemy siege. Additionally, the Texans dug a well within the Alamo's walls to ensure that they would have a constant and reliable water supply, and used the excavated earth to make last-minute repairs and build more fortifications on which to mount their cannons [1].

All told, the Alamo was defended by 18 cannons, and a small but fiercely determined band of 150 Texans and Tejanos [12]. Over half of their number were under the age of thirty, and included many youths who had not yet reached the age of twenty [19]. On the other hand, Santa Anna's army was rumored to be numbered in the thousands, and was well disciplined, trained, and thoroughly equipped [3].

The Mexican army did not waste any time in taking possession of the now abandoned town of San Antonio de Bexar and swiftly commenced their preparations for the siege. As soon as they were free to do so, Ben, Mary, and several of the Texans mounted the Alamo's walls to observe their movements. "Ben," Mary said suddenly, after they had been quietly standing and watching together for some time, "What is the meaning of that red flag over the Bexar church? Is it a signal of some sort?" At first, Ben did not reply, and Mary, thinking he might not have heard her, turned to look up at him. She saw that his jaw was clenched tightly, and noticed that his eyes held a strange look that she had not seen before. At last, he drew a deep breath and put his arm protectingly around her shoulders. "It means 'No Quarter,' Sis." He answered in a low voice. Mary started slightly. "You mean they do not intend to — to show mercy to anyone?" She exclaimed. "I'm afraid so, Mary." He replied sadly, as he saw the look of horror that filled her face. "If, God forbid, the enemy successfully overthrows our stronghold... they will not hesitate to put all of her defenders to the sword." "Dear God!" she murmured, and as the full meaning of his words sank in, Ben felt a shudder run through her slight frame as she clung all the more closely to him.

Before long, the sound of a bugle was heard, and a white flag was run up over the Mexican lines. At this, Colonels Travis and Bowie hastened to join the men on the wall to evaluate the situation. "Do you suppose they are surrenderin' to us, Colonel Bowie?" One of the Texan defenders quipped, as Bowie observed the white flag and the movements of the Mexican army through his spyglass. "Not hardly." Bowie answered grimly. "If I am not mistaken, Santa Anna intends to parlay with us, although I cannot imagine what the dickens he could want." "Regardless, we must find out." Travis responded shortly, and promptly ordered one of the Texans to mount and ride out to receive the message under the protection of a white flag. The men on the wall watched as the messenger rode off towards San Antonio de Bexar, and quietly discussed their expectations about the message he would bring back to them. They hadn't long to wait, for the messenger could soon be seen galloping back bearing a letter from Santa Anna's aide. After reaching the protection of the Alamo, he swiftly dismounted, and hurried up the wall to deliver the message to Travis. The Texans quickly gathered around the spot as Travis proceeded to open and read the letter. "Well, Travis?" Bowie exclaimed impatiently, breaking the long moment of silence that ensued. Travis folded up the message, and handed it to Bowie. "In short, Santa Anna is offering us terms of surrender at discretion." He stated curtly, "He has declared that our best hope is to place ourselves in the hands of the 'Supreme Mexican

Government', and surrender to the fate that he has determined for us." "As if we would be so weak and cowardly as to give ourselves up!" Scoffed Bowie as he crumbled up the message and tossed it over the wall, turning back to face Travis and the men who had gathered around them. "Surrender is unthinkable! It is far better to stand and die fighting, rather than to submit, and be cut down and trodden underfoot at the whim of such a despotic tyrant. Am I not right, men?" And all who heard this stern declaration promptly answered with a loud roar of assent. "So be it!" Travis declared, fierce determination flashing in his eyes, "Boys, charge up the eighteen-pounder! Let us send Santa Anna a message that will make our resolve all the more clear to him!" The men hastened to obey the order, and as soon as the cannon was ready, and Travis gave the word, they fired the cannon, and to their grim pleasure, the loud boom and explosion that followed seemed to cause quite a stir in the enemy quarter.

Soon thereafter, infuriated at the defiance of the Texan rebels, the Mexican army commenced their siege of the Alamo. They began their bombardment using light field cannons, which, because of their shorter firing range, forced them to come quite close to the old mission, and consequently within range of the Texan's long rifles. For the rest of that long first day, Ben and the other men were busily occupied with picking off as many of the enemy as they could, specifically targeting those working the field cannons. They soon wreaked such havoc upon the Mexican soldiers that they were forced to dig trenches to provide themselves with some shelter [4], and because of these efforts, their attack was slightly subdued for a time. Ben stayed close to Colonel Crockett all throughout the day and was astonished when he witnessed the accuracy of his aim. When he chanced to make a remark about this, Crockett replied with a laugh, "All's I can tell you Drury is that this is not the first fight Old Betsy here has seen. You see, I've been kind o' forced to get well practiced at this here business over the course of my lifetime in order to keep from being killed." After a slight pause, he added, "You're not such a bad shot yourself, though, Son — did you have similar schooling?" "Fortunately, no," Ben said with a grin as he reloaded his piece, "I got my practice by keeping pesky varmints from overrunning my family's farm, and also from hunting." "That certainly is a safer way to l'arn," Crockett answered as he raised his rifle to his shoulder, "For at least in that case, the critters won't be a' shootin' back at you!"

During this time, Mary, with the help of Suzanna and a few of the other women, worked to treat the minor injuries that a few of the Texans had sustained. When she was not needed for this, she and the other women busied themselves with preparing simple rations for the men. These they usually came to retrieve in shifts, so as to never leave the walls of the Alamo undefended. As darkness came on, the hostilities came to somewhat of a halt, allowing for a brief reprieve on both sides. Despite this,

Travis ordered sentries to be posted at intervals along the walls to keep up a constant vigil throughout the night, in order to prevent any surprise attacks from the enemy.

The dawn of the next morning brought little cheer, for not only were the hostilities renewed once again with a vengeance, but Mary also received an alarming summons concerning Colonel Bowie, who had been suddenly smitten with violent illness. Bowie had taken a heavy fall from some scaffolding a couple of days prior while trying to direct the placement of a cannon, but as he had been able to go about his duties as usual for some time afterwards, he gave little thought to his injuries. However, on the second day of the siege, he came down with a terrific high fever, which confined him to his bed [1]. Mary did all within her power to ease the man's sufferings and went to nurse him often throughout the day. Despite all of her efforts, Bowie's illness became so severe that he was forced to hand over the total command of the Alamo to Travis — something that he was very reluctant to do.

"How is Colonel Bowie, Mary?" Ben queried when he came down from his position on the wall for his meager evening rations. "Not too well, Ben," she replied. "He has an awful fever, and is even becoming slightly delirious. I'm doing all that I can, but I don't have all the medical supplies that I need,

BEN MANAGED TO STAY CLOSE TO COLONEL CROCKETT ALL THROUGHOUT THE DAY

which limits the extent of what I can do." Dejectedly, Ben sat down on a bit of broken wall, his face clouded with a look of mingled weariness and discouragement. "What is troubling you, Ben?" Mary asked, coming to stand beside him and resting her hand on his shoulder. "Oh Mary," He answered, looking up at her with a sad smile, "I was only wishing that you were a thousand miles away from this place. Up there on the walls, I could see the area around us for miles, and Mary, it's covered with nothing but enemy soldiers as far as the eye can see! We are like a tiny little scrap of an island surrounded on every side by raging seas, ready to crush us into oblivion." Mary was very quiet for moment. "Do you think there is any hope of help coming through to us, Ben?" She asked him at last, "I sure hope so, Sis," He replied solemnly. "I can't imagine how any freedom-loving man could ignore our situation here. Colonel Travis has sent messengers to both Goliad and Gonzales, as you well know, and he is certain that as soon as enough men can be mustered together, they will move heaven and earth to come and relieve us." Both siblings fell quiet once again for several moments as they pondered their situation. Mary was the first to break the silence. "Remember," she said, "That passage in the Psalms that mother always used to recite to us when we were afraid? 'God is our refuge and strength, a very present help in a time of trouble—therefore we shall not fear.' [5] God will be our strength, Ben dear, no matter what happens." "Indeed He will Mary," Ben replied, taking her small hand in his, "And to be quite frank, our Lord is and always will be the one and only true hope that we have."

As soon as Ben finished his hasty meal, he made his way to Colonel Travis' quarters to report about several important observations he had made concerning their defensive position. Upon reaching his destination, he knocked on the door, and then stood waiting for permission to enter. "Come in!" He heard a rather muffled voice call at last, and quickly opening the door, he stepped into the Colonel's quarters. Travis was busily writing at his desk, but he looked up momentarily as Ben walked over to him. "Good evening, Drury," He said, as he went on with his work, "Would you happen to know where my aide, Sergeant Bennington is? I have a message that I need him to deliver at once." "I haven't seen him recently, Sir," Ben replied respectfully, "But I believe he might be found over by the entrenchments in front of the old chapel. Last I heard, he was helping to direct the construction of some new fortifications there." "I must send for him at once," Travis said, rising from his seat and coming around to the front of his desk, "I have just written an appeal that is directed to all the citizens of Texas, as well as to our American brethren. I related our situation here, and our resolve to hold firm at all costs, and — there, seeing as you are my trusted friend as well as my best scout, I might as well just read it to you and let you hear it for yourself." The Colonel turned to pick up the letter and then sat down on the edge of his desk.

Commandancy of the The Alamo
Bejar, Feby. 24th. 1836

To the People of Texas and All Americans in the World-
Fellow Citizens and compatriots-
*I am besieged, by a thousand or more of the Mexicans under Santa Anna - I have sustained a continual Bombardment and cannonade for 24 hours and have not lost a man - The enemy has demanded a surrender at discretion, otherwise, the garrison are to be put to the sword, if the fort is taken - I have answered the demand with a cannon shot, and our flag still waves proudly from the walls - I shall never surrender or retreat. Then, I call on you in the name of Liberty, of patriotism and everything dear to the American character, to come to our aid, with all dispatch - The enemy is receiving reinforcements daily and will no doubt increase to three or four thousand in four or five days. If this call is neglected, I am determined to sustain myself as long as possible and die like a soldier who never forgets what is due to his own honor and that of his country - **Victory or Death**.*
Signed,
William Barret Travis.
Lt. Col.comdt.

P. S. The Lord is on our side - When the enemy appeared in sight we had not three bushels of corn - We have since found in deserted houses 80 or 90 bushels and got into the walls 20 or 30 head of Beeves.

Travis [6]

"Well Drury," Travis said after a brief pause as he folded up his missive, "What do you think?" "What do I think, Sir?" Ben exclaimed eagerly, "I say that if I were not already here, alongside you and all the other Texans within these walls, I could not resist such an entreaty! I thank you for reading me your letter, for I will admit that I was feeling rather despondent and doubtful of any aid being sent to us. But I can't see how anyone could resist the bold appeal in your letter, especially when they learn of the desperate nature of our situation." "I understand your discouragement, Drury," Travis said, looking down at the letter in his hand, "And I know that the welfare of your sister must be weighing heavily on your mind. But take heart in the assurance that the Lord is with us. He has supplied our needs and strengthened our hand all throughout this ordeal, and we know He will continue to do so, regardless of what lies ahead." "Yes Sir," Ben acknowledged reverently.

"However," Travis continued, "I am certain that help will come before too much longer, if only we can hold out until it arrives." "Indeed we shall, Sir," Ben replied, "And it is regarding our defense that I have come here to speak with you. When I was last on the walls, I noticed some wooden sheds located just a few yards away on the other side. Colonel Crockett and I were discussing the possibility of making a sortie this evening to destroy them, and perhaps even retrieving some lumber from them for scaffolding. Those sheds are so close to the walls that the enemy could use them as cover when they begin their advance, which would make it extremely difficult for us to drive them out again." The Colonel sighed. "We should have attended to them sooner." He said gravely, "Very well Drury, you and Crockett may proceed with your sortie this evening. However, I must ask that you use extreme caution and ensure that you do not take any unnecessary risks, for we cannot afford to lose any of our fighting men." "Yes Sir!" Ben answered with alacrity, and after saluting Travis, he hastened to take his departure.

At about eleven o'clock that evening, Crockett, Ben, and a few other men made their sortie. They slipped quietly out of the Alamo and were successfully able to make their way to the sheds without being observed. Once there, they proceeded to strip whatever planking that they could salvage from the dilapidated buildings, which they then swiftly transported back to the Alamo while the rest of the men set fire to the now useless remains. They worked so quickly and efficiently, that before the Mexican army realized what had happened, the old structures were thoroughly ablaze, and the small band of men who had accomplished the deed were once again safe inside the walls of the old mission. The Texans were much heartened by this small expedition, and wasted no time in setting up scaffolding in various partitions of the Alamo for the advantage of the sharpshooters.

The next morning, however, the situation took another dark turn for the defenders of the Alamo. The Mexican troops began attempting to close in upon them, and endeavored to set up a battery in front of the Alamo's gate, a movement which the Texans discouraged with their heavy fire while daylight lasted. After nightfall, it was a different story. The Mexicans took the advantage of the darkness and some buildings that were located between the river and the Alamo, and using them as cover for their movements, they set up their guns within distance of about 300 yards of the old mission's gate [1]. That same night, Crockett and Ben once again took a small detachment of men to burn down the treacherous structures. They were subjected to heavy enemy fire, but they stubbornly persisted in their efforts, and successfully managed to destroy quite a number of the buildings. However, by this time, the Mexicans were deeply entrenched in their new position, and not only were they able to finish setting up their batteries by morning, but their cavalry also began blocking off the road to Gonzales to more completely isolate the Alamo. They were now close enough to engage with any of the Texans who happened to be outside the walls of the Alamo, which forced the latter to confine themselves more closely than ever to the protection of the old mission [1].

Day after day, the situation continued to become more and more desperate as more Mexican troops arrived, and the enemy continued to press in even harder upon the Texans. All this time, their batteries continued to get closer to the defender's position, while the heavy bombardment steadily increased and pounded away at the mission's ancient walls. The Texans were now running dangerously low on ammunition, and as a result, they did the best they could to conserve the little that they had left for the full-scale enemy assault [1]. Travis continued to send messages pleading for reinforcements, even appealing to General Sam Houston, though the latter was in desperate straights himself, having nothing but a very small and poorly equipped army. *"Do hasten on aid to me as rapidly as possible,"* Travis wrote, *"As from the superior number of the enemy, it will be impossible for us to keep them out much longer. If they overpower us, we fall a sacrifice at the shrine of our country, and we hope prosperity and our country will do our memory justice. Give me help, oh my country! Victory or Death!"* [17]

About a week into the siege, James Bonham, one of Travis' messengers, slipped out of the Alamo to meet up with James Fannin, the commander of the Texan force at Goliad, whom Travis had sent for soon after the Mexicans had first arrived. Travis expected that by this time Fannin and his men must be very close by, and hoped that Bonham could find him and persuade him to hasten with all speed to their aid. After two days had gone by, and neither Bonham nor Fannin made their appearance, Travis sent out yet another messenger, a Mexican by the name of Captain Juan Seguin, accompanied by his nephew, to try and find Fannin, and bring him and his men to the relief of the Alamo [1].

While the siege at the Alamo continued unabated, and unbeknownst to the Texas defenders, over a hundred miles away, on the evening of March 1, 1836, Texas delegates met together on Washington-on-the-Brazos, and drafted the Texas Declaration of Independence. Up until that point, they had withheld from taking the irrevocable step of separating from Mexico, seeking to leave room for a peaceful solution to resolve the conflict. However, after witnessing Santa Anna's cruel and relentless attacks upon the people of Texas, most notably through his merciless attack upon their comrades the Alamo, the Texan delegates recognized Santa Anna's determination to utterly crush them and their cause for freedom, and realized that the time for their separation from Mexico had arrived. At last, on the following day, March 2, 1836, the Texas Declaration of Independence was unanimously approved and signed, thus finally establishing Texas as an independent nation. How long that independence would last, however, was a question that only time would tell [10].

Back at the Alamo, on the night of March 1, Ben was standing listlessly at the mission walls, taking his turn at sentry duty. The lack of sleep and intense stress was telling severely upon all the men, and Ben was feeling both jaded and anxious. What had become of Fannin, Bonham, and Seguin? Would help ever arrive, or would they simply be left to be slaughtered by Santa Anna's murderous henchmen? And what on earth would become of Mary if that were to be the case? Ben sighed and leaned wearily against the wall at this last thought, which weighed more heavily upon him than any of the others. "Hello thar', Drury. How are you holdin' up?" Crockett asked as he came to join Ben on the wall. "Is that you Davy?" Ben answered, turning momentarily to greet his friend before returning his gaze to the dark expanse before him, "Oh, I guess I'm just hanging on, like everyone else is. Though it's not making me feel any better, I've also been doing a lot of thinking while trying to keep myself awake." "I see." Crockett said, as he leaned against the wall and stared off into the distance, "I've been doin' some serious thinkin' myself these past few days. I suppose a man can't help but do so when under these circumstances. Were you a' wonderin' about Fannin and his men?" "I was," Ben replied downheartedly. "So much time has passed, and I would have thought that help would have come through by now. Do you think that something must've happened to them?" "I don't reckon I know, Ben, it's impossible to say." Crockett answered gravely. The two men stood in a thoughtful silence for quite some time, listening to the night sounds of the Texas wilderness, intently alert for any movements from the enemy quarter. Finally, Ben's relief came, and they started on their way back to the barracks. A startled cry and the report of a rifle from the newly arrived sentry instantly arrested their departure, and Ben and Crockett rushed back to the wall with all of the speed that they could muster. "What on earth ails you, Man?" Cried Crockett as soon as he reached the spot where the sentry stood, who was hastily reloading his rifle, "I saw a body of men approaching from right out there, Sir!" The man pointed in the direction indicated with a shaking finger, "It's must be the Mexicans preparing for an attack!" He would have fired his rifle again had not Crockett arrested his movements. "Wait a minute thar'!" He exclaimed, "Are you certain it was the enemy?" All at once, a loud cry sounded from below. "Hold your fire!" the voice yelled. "We are reinforcements from Gonzales! Open the gate for heaven's sake before we are discovered!"

With a cry of joy, Ben leaped down from the wall and joined the growing throng of men at the Alamo's gate. As soon as it was opened, thirty-two men filed in through the gate, and were received with a warm welcome by the Texans. The defenders of the Alamo were nearly wild with joy at the arrival of these new reinforcements, and it took some time for their commanding officers to restore order again. After they had calmed down sufficiently, the newly arrived reinforcements informed their comrades that they had come through the enemy lines alone to join them in their desperate stand. When news had first arrived in Gonzales regarding the plight at the Alamo, they had immediately made their preparations for departure. They expected that a force would immediately be rallied together to go to the relief of Travis and his men, but to their dismay, no such occurrence took place. At last, these thirty-two brave souls began the dangerous journey to the Alamo on their own. They knew that their tiny band wouldn't make a significant difference in the desperate situation their comrades were in, but they also knew that they could not sit idly by and leave them to fight and die alone [1].

As small as this reinforcement was, it did much to hearten the defenders of the Alamo. Surely Fannin could not be far behind, they thought, and when the reinforcements he brought arrived, they would then route the enemy, and give them such a hiding as they would never forget! With their hope and determination thus renewed, they settled in to wait for Fannin's arrival. The two days that followed were much the same as those preceding them, except that reinforcements for the Mexican army continued to arrive, and the last obscure inroads leading to the Alamo were discovered and blocked off, rendering the Texans completely isolated and still more hopelessly outnumbered than before [1].

Late on the morning of the second day, the sentries on the walls of the Alamo caught sight of a lone rider racing towards their position, under the hot pursuit of an enemy patrol. Upon hearing the news, the defenders rushed to the walls to offer whatever cover they could to this strange horseman, who, as he drew nearer, was recognized as Bonham. Against all odds, he had managed to slip through the Mexican lines, and, though heavily pursued, he went on at a breakneck speed to reach the Alamo with his message. Thanks to the protective fire from his comrades, his pursuing foes were driven back, and before long, he was safe inside the mission and dismounting from his horse, breathing heavily from the chase. As soon as he had received word of his messenger's return, Travis hurried from his quarters and joined the group of men surrounding Bonham. "Well, man, what tidings do you bring? Where are Fannin and his men?" He exclaimed as soon as he could make himself heard. For a moment, Bonham just stared at Travis as if he had not heard him, while all the men gathered around them grew very silent, anxiously awaiting his reply. Finally, Bonham made a despairing gesture, and answered in a hoarse voice, "I am sorry Sir... but there is no help coming. Not from Fannin, or from anyone else."

Footnotes:

[1] Warren, R. (1958.) *Remember the Alamo!* Random House, Inc.

[4] Giorello, J. (2016.) *Bunker Hill to WWI: Great Battles for Boys.* Rolling Wheel Publishing.

[5] (New King James Version, 1996, Psalm 46:1)

[6] The Alamo. (n.d.) *Travis Letter: Victory or Death.* Retrieved from: https://www.thealamo.org/remember/battle-and-revolution/travis-letter

[12] TheAlamo.org. (n.d). *Battle and Revolution: Freedoms Worth Fighting For.* Retrieved from: https://www.thealamo.org/remember/battle-and-revolution

Chapter 6

Line in the Sand

To this day, there is much uncertainty as to why Fannin failed to come to the relief of the defenders of the Alamo. After receiving Travis' message, he had started with his men for the Alamo, but just outside of Goliad, one of his supply wagons broke down, and he turned back with his men to Goliad. When Captain Seguin arrived in Goliad and heard the story of this retreat from Fannin's officers, he rode on to Gonzales in an endeavor to rally enforcements. However, despite his efforts, other than the thirty-two brave men who had traveled to the Alamo alone, no other reinforcements were sent, leaving the Alamo to be defended by just over one hundred and eighty men against Santa Anna's thousands [1].

Bonham's devastating declaration was met by the men of the Alamo with an awful silence. Stunned, the Texans looked about at each other with looks of shock and desperation as the terrible truth of their situation sank in. Ben, who had joined the group just before Bonham related his grim tidings, had grown as white as a sheet. Davy Crockett was standing beside him, and upon seeing Ben's countenance, he quietly and unobtrusively took him by the arm and guided him away from the crowd. As soon as they were out of earshot, Crockett said, "Ben, I reckon it'd be best for your sister to hear the news from you a'fore it reaches her from another source. You could break it to her sort of gentle-like, and talk things over with her... just as soon as you get ahold o' yourself, that is." "Yes — yes, I know ." Ben replied shortly, and pulling himself free from Crockett, he walked swiftly away towards the chapel. Before he reached it, Crockett watched him stop suddenly, turn, and walk off with his head hung low toward the old plaza, where he soon stopped to lean heavily against the walls of the long barracks.

Crockett silently followed, and upon reaching Ben, he too leaned up against the wall beside him. "Davy, what on earth am I going to do with Mary?" Ben exclaimed at last, dejectedly, "I don't care about what happens to me, it's just that I was a fool to allow Mary to stay here, and I simply cannot just stand by and allow her to join in my fate... but what can I do?" Crockett shifted slightly, and met Ben's distress-filled gaze. "I've been doin' some figurin' Ben," he said quietly, "And I think we could move the women folks and their youngins' into the partition in the back o' the old chapel. We could leave them a good supply o' vittles and water, and then barricade the door. They will be a good deal safer that way from all the firing, and who knows? Maybe the Mexicans will spare them, seein' that they are helpless and ain't been involved in the fighting." "Perhaps you're right Davy." Ben said, brightening up slightly, "Do you really think that Santa Anna would spare them?" "There's no sayin' for sure, Ben, but then again, there is always the slight chance that he might." "Then we'd better to get to work right away, before it is too late!" Ben cried, straightening up as he spoke. "You're right there, lad," Crockett replied, "Why don't you go have a talk with your sister while I speak to some of the other men? After that, we can begin our preparations." Ben nodded in agreement, and with a smothered sigh, he started off swiftly on his errand. Despite all of his attempts to recover his composure, he was still reeling inwardly from Bonham's tidings. Though Crockett's plan to provide safety for the women and children had brought him some comfort, the thought of his little sister being left all alone and unprotected in the world distressed him greatly. How he dreaded having to relay such terrible tidings to her!

All too soon, Ben reached the old chapel, and after pausing, irresolute, at the threshold, he opened the door softly and quietly entered. The first sight that met his eyes was Mary, fully absorbed with caring for the wounded men, who now filled nearly half of the non-too roomy expanse. He stood in the doorway for several moments, watching her move to and fro, offering a gentle word, soothing a feverish forehead, or giving a cool drink of water to whoever requested it. At last, she chanced to look up from her work and noticed her brother, and immediately hurried over to him, a glad smile upon her face. "Mary," He said somewhat abruptly as soon as she was close enough, "Do you have a moment? I must speak with you concerning an urgent matter." "Certainly, Ben,"

She answered hesitatingly, anxiously searching his face, "Only I mustn't stray too far off in case one of my patients should need me." She led Ben to the same partition in the back of the old chapel that he and Crockett had been speaking about just a few moments before, so that they could converse in private. Once they were both inside, Ben closed the makeshift door, and on sudden impulse, he put his arms about Mary in a hearty, brotherly embrace, and then drew her down to sit beside him on some old broken boxes. "My dear little sister," He said at last, "I have done you a great wrong." "Why, whatever do you mean, Ben? You haven't wronged me in any way!" Mary exclaimed indignantly. "Indeed I have, sis," He answered sadly. "It was in that I allowed you to remain here with me, instead of sending you with Dr. Dopkins, where you would have been safe. Mary, Bonham just returned about half an hour ago with the news that there will be no help coming to us from Fannin, or anyone. We don't know exactly why, though it is true that the Texan army is very small in number, leaving Houston in very tight straits with no men to spare. Regardless, it is now quite evident that our meager force here at the Alamo will be left to stand alone against Santa Anna and his army. As the odds are overwhelmingly against us, we have no hope of holding them off on our own... and I know that you realize what that means for us, dear." In the silence that followed his words, Ben took his little sister's hand in his and waited for her to speak. He had expected that Mary would be terribly shocked at this piece of unexpected news, but except that her face grew rather pale, and her grip on his hand tightened, she didn't seem to be much altered, or dismayed. "I see." She said at last in a low voice. "Colonel Crockett and I were just discussing what could be done to protect non-combatants such as yourself," Ben continued, "And we believe that if all the women and children take shelter in this very back room, we could barricade the door, and then you would all be out of immediate danger when the full scale assault takes place. We are fairly certain that when you are eventually discovered, the enemy will most likely spare all of you. I know it's not much of a chance, but I'm afraid it's the only option we have left." "But they certainly will not spare any of the men, will they, Ben?" Mary asked, meeting his eyes in a searching gaze. "I'm afraid not, sis." He answered quietly.

Mary hastily rose to her feet and walked to the other end of the room. For a moment, she just stood there with her back to him, and her hands clasped tightly together. At last, she turned around to face him, and as soon as Ben caught sight of the look on her face, he knew that there was going to be trouble. "Ben," Mary said, in a firm, clear voice, "I am ever so grateful to you for everything you have done to care for and protect me, and I greatly appreciate what you and Colonel Crockett are planning to do to protect those as defenseless as myself. But dear brother, there is work I firmly believe God has sent me here to do —

and that is to care for any of the defenders of this mission who are wounded in our stand for freedom. Just think, Ben, not all wounds incapacitate their victims, and it may be that I might be able to patch up such individuals well enough as to enable them to return to their posts. As for those who are too severely wounded, I will tend to them as best as I am able, and do all within my power to lead those of them who do not know their Savior to salvation, so that when they pass from this life to the next, they shall go to spend eternity with Him." "But Mary!" Ben exclaimed, leaping to his feet. "Such acts could very well get you killed! Why, it would be seen as aiding and abetting the enemy! You could also just as easily be struck down by a stray bullet, or be murdered before Santa Anna's army realizes you are but a helpless woman!" "I fully realize that, Ben," Mary said, striving to maintain her composure, "Do please try to calm yourself and listen to me. You know fully well that you cannot make me go against my conscience, and I know I could never live with myself if I left the patients that have been entrusted to my care to be slaughtered." Ben was now pacing up and down the room like a wild animal in a cage. "And what do you expect to do when Santa Anna's army breaks into this chapel? Do you really think that you could stop them from killing your patients?" "Why, of course not, Ben. In that case, the only thing we could do would be to attempt to defend ourselves for as long as possible." "What on earth — do you mean that you actually intend to take part in their defense,

Mary?" "Would you rather that I stand by quietly and wait for my end while I watch my patients get butchered, Ben? If you will please allow me to finish," — "No! I cannot permit you to do this thing!" Ben cried fiercely. "You must remain where you will be safe, and I will not listen to any other argument for otherwise!" With that, Ben made a stormy exit from the room. For a moment, Mary stood and watched the retreating form of her brother as he strode through the old chapel towards the door. "Father in heaven, I pray that you will soften Ben's heart, and help him understand as only you can," she prayed softly, "For it seems as though I have only made a mess of things."

Ben hurried back to the long barracks, his mind in an absolute turmoil. He had expected that Mary might be slightly opposed to his plan, but he had never dreamed that she would be so firmly set upon refusing to comply with it. Whatever was he to do with her now? Ben knew Mary well enough to know that once she made her mind up about something she believed to be right, it was next to impossible to persuade her to change it. "Perhaps," he thought, after his anger had somewhat subsided, "She will listen to Crockett, for she respects him more than any other individual I know of." With this thought in mind, Ben wasted no time setting about the search for his friend, whom he presently found directing a small group of men who were busily occupied with gathering provisions that were to be taken to the non-combatant's place of refuge. As soon as he was able, Crockett hurried over to Ben. "Well lad, how did your talk go over with your sister?" He queried. "Not very well at all Davy," Ben replied with a frustrated jester, "She insists upon staying with the wounded to the last, and even talked of some foolish notion of attempting to defend them!" "Is that so?" Responded Crockett in amazement, with something of a smile. "I'm afraid it is Davy, and her determination is so firmly set that I am at a loss as to what I should do. I thought perhaps you could try to talk to her, for she has the utmost respect for you and might listen to what you have to say." Crockett scratched his head, looking rather uncertain. "I don't know Ben, I ain't of much use at that thar' sort of business, but I reckon I could give it a shot for both of your sakes." "Thank you Davy, I'll take you to her." Ben answered gratefully and hastened to lead the Colonel to his sister.

When they reached the outside of the old chapel, they saw Mary with Susanna Dickinson, and noticed that both young women were heavily laden with supplies, which they assumed they must be taking to store for the use of the women and children. The two men silently followed the women at a distance through the chapel, and stopped just outside the back room to wait for them to come out again. "I hope that this room will hold all of us." They heard Suzanna say to Mary as the two girls carefully stowed away their burdens. "Oh, I'm sure it will, Suzanna," The latter replied, "And you will most likely hardly notice if your quarters are cramped, once the fighting starts." "You speak as though you will not be here with us!" Suzanna said suddenly, stopping her work to look at her friend. Mary also paused to briefly meet her gaze. "It is true," she answered quietly, "I have resolved to stay with my patients. There will be even more wounded in need of medical attention once the battle begins again, and there is no one else here to look after them in my stead." "Oh Mary, you could not think of doing such a thing!" Cried Suzanna in horror, "You will surely be murdered, and of what good will your death be? Besides, there is your brother — have you not thought of him, and how he will feel about this?" Mary walked over to her friend, and placed a gentle hand on her arm. "I have thought of these things Suzanna," she said simply, "And there is something that I must tell you. Somehow, from the very day that we first spent in this place, I had a very strong feeling that we might never be permitted to leave it in peace again. I don't know how or why, but it was a feeling that I could not shake off. It bothered me a great deal at first... especially whenever I thought about the fate the enemy promised us. All the while, I kept asking myself how I might best use the remainder of my life to serve my Lord and my country. After considerable contemplation and prayer, I have come to believe that is God's will for me to use my skills as a battlefield nurse to render whatever assistance that I can to the brave men here, who are making such a gallant stand for the independence of Texas. I fully realize that such a step will most likely cost me my life, but how can I hide away in safety when I know that I could perhaps be helping to save a life, or sending a soldier back into battle? Despite the heavy odds against us, we may hold out for quite some time yet, and every moment that we delay Santa Anna and his army will be precious to General Houston. To do this, Suzanna, every man who is well enough to continue fighting will be needed, and in a small way, I can help to fulfill this need — for a time at least." She paused for a moment, and Suzanna saw her dark eyes fill with tears as she went on again. "I will admit that I prefer death to going on alone in the world without Ben. But something that troubles me even more that this is the thought of all of my patients — those courageous souls, lying helpless, and alone here, with no one to stand in their defense when Santa Anna's murderous troops storm this place. I know they will be shown no mercy, and will be put to the sword regardless of anything that I might do. But even though I am but a woman, I would far rather be killed caring for them in any way that I can, then to live out the rest of my days, and one day stand before my Savior knowing that I willingly left them to be slaughtered." For a moment, Suzanna just stood and looked at Mary, speechless from the weight and passion of her words. The next instant, both girls were in each other's arms, mingling their tears freely together. "Oh Mary, dear, dear Mary!" Suzanna sobbed, "How I wish I could stay with you!" Mary did her best to soothe her friend despite her own tears. "I know you would Suzanna," she said, "But your child will need her mother, and you know that it gives your husband peace of mind to know that you will both be safe."

Ben looked over at Crockett, and the latter motioned to Ben to follow him as he exited the chapel. Once outside, Crockett turned to look squarely into his face. "Ben," He said gravely, "You should be mighty proud to have a sister with such courage, for there ain't many women with that kind of grit. I'm afraid you're a'goin' to have to pardon me, because there just ain't no way that I can speak to her now, after hearin' her convictions on the subject. I'm no saint myself, but I know that it is downright sinful to try to persuade somebody to go against their conscience." "I know Davy. I wouldn't ask you to — not after hearing how strongly Mary feels." Ben replied somewhat hoarsely, for he was having difficulty controlling a sudden lump that had risen in his throat. Crockett saw the anguished look in his young friend's eyes, and rested one of his large, calloused hands upon his shoulder. "I'm sorry Ben," He said quietly, "I wish that there were somethin' that I could do to help... but you see how things stand." Ben shook his head, and answered in a low voice, "I'm just sorry that I was so mule-headed, letting my frustration get the better of me and not giving Mary a chance to explain... She sure is a swell little sister, and I — I couldn't be prouder of her." At this, Crockett grinned slightly, and nodded his head in agreement. "Make sure that you tell her that." He said pointedly.

For the next hour, the defenders were busy at work completing their preparations for the women and children, and it was quite some time before Ben had any opportunity to talk with Mary. He occasionally caught sight of her as he worked, and it brought him great sorrow to see how troubled and saddened she looked whenever she glanced in his direction. Just as the men were finishing their various tasks, Colonel Travis' appearance on the scene arrested their movements. "I apologize for the interruption men," He said in a loud clear voice, so that all might hear him, "But I must have a word with you all before the lull in the bombardment ends. Please meet me in the plaza within five minutes; I shall join you there as soon as I have gathered the other men." As soon as Travis had left, the men made their way to the said meeting place, talking quietly amongst themselves as they went. "What do you suppose the Colonel wishes to talk with us about Davy?" Ben asked as he walked alongside his companion. "I don't rightly know, Ben," Crockett replied soberly, "But if I were to guess, I'd imagine it's goin' to be about Bonham's news, and what our response should be."

Before long, the defenders of the Alamo were gathered in the old mission's plaza. Even Colonel Bowie, sick as he was, had insisted upon being with them, and was carried out on his cot and set in their midst. They were soon joined by their commander, Colonel Travis, and he wasted no time in getting straight to the point of what he wanted to say to them. "As I am sure many of you must have already guessed," He began, "I have called you here in order to relate the exact circumstances of our situation. Just as you heard Bonham say, there will be no one coming to our aid. I know I don't have to tell you what that means for all of us here, as the enemy has already made their intent on that score plain enough. You have gone above and beyond your call of duty, staying here despite the overwhelming odds and holding off the enemy for well over a week's time." He paused for a moment and scanned the faces of the men about him. "I have resolved stay and defend our stronghold to the last," He went on, "But I do not ask any of you to stay here and die with me who would rather attempt to escape while there is yet time. No one can blame any of you who desires to do so, the least of which being myself. Indeed, I am honored to have been permitted to have the privilege of commanding such fine men."

Travis broke off suddenly, and drawing his sword, he turned and walked a short distance from the Texans. The men watched in silence as he used it to draw a well-defined line in the sandy soil. "Any man who wishes to stay," he called as soon as he had finished, "Let him join me on the opposite side of this line." For a moment, the men stood in silence, and exchanged questioning glances with each other as the full weight of Travis's words sank in. What course should they choose? All at once, there was a movement from the back of the crowd. "Step aside, if you please, boys!" The loud, clear voice of Davy Crockett rang out, and before anyone fully realized what was happening, he had made his way through the throng, and without hesitation strode across the line in the sand to stand beside Travis. Ben was the first to follow his example, and before long, the entire group of Texans began making their way across the line to join their brave commander. Colonel Bowie called out feebly to the men who had already crossed over, and asked if they would help him across, a request which several of them hurried to fulfill, and he was soon carefully borne over the line.

Ben stood on the outside of the throng of defenders who had rallied around Travis, solemnly watching as his brave comrades continued to cross the line in the sand to join them. He was slightly startled when he felt a small hand slip through his arm, and when he looked down, his eyes fell on Mary's upturned face. Her eyes were brimming with unshed tears, but they also shone with love and pride. "May God bless you, my dear brother." She said softly. He in response rested his hand gently on hers, and replied, "He already has Mary, by giving me such a brave little sister as you."

"ANY MAN WHO WISHES TO STAY, LET HIM JOIN ME ON THE OPPOSITE SIDE OF THIS LINE."

Chapter 7

Ben

The rest of the day was very trying to the inhabitants of the Alamo, especially since everyone was now fully aware of the inevitable fate that awaited them. It was heartbreaking to behold the distress of the women and children as they bid their final farewells to their husbands, fathers, brothers, or sons when the time came for them to take refuge in the small back room in the chapel. Many of the men seemed hardly able to tear themselves away from their loved ones, knowing that they most likely would never see them again. However, there were also men who did not have any family with them in the old fortress, and these spent the remainder of the lull in the hostilities writing letters of farewell to their families or friends, hoping and praying that their messages would somehow reach them. Travis himself wrote a letter to one of his superiors, the president of the Washington Convention for Texas Independence [1], detailing their situation. He closed by saying, *"I feel confident that the determined valor heretofore exhibited by my men will not fail them in the last struggle. The victory will cost the enemy so dear that it will be worse for him than defeat... The power of Santa Anna is to be met here or in the colonies; we had better meet them here, than to suffer a war of desolation to rage our settlements. A blood-red banner waves from the church of Bexar, and in the camp above us, in token that the war is one of vengeance against rebels; they have declared us as such, and demanded that we should surrender at discretion or this garrison should be put to the sword. Their threats have had no influence on me or my men, but to make all fight with desperation, and that high-souled courage which characterizes the patriot, who is willing to die in defense of his country's liberty and his own honor* [17]." This precious missive, together with other letters from the Alamo's defenders were entrusted to a messenger, and the latter departed on his errand as soon as a safe opportunity was afforded to him.

In his spare time, Ben set about acquiring certain necessary provisions for Mary, also managing to procure a several long rifles and a rather scanty store of ammunition for her use. "It may be," He said when she inquired as to why he had brought her more than one firearm, "That some of the wounded men under your care will be well enough to help you defend this place, and you will be able to hold out much longer with their assistance if that is the case." "I had not thought of that," she replied in a low voice, "And I hope for their sakes that there will not be many left utterly defenseless." "So do I, Mary." Ben answered sadly, "For I am afraid that when that time comes, you will have a hot time of it here. If we fail to keep the enemy back, and Santa Anna's men are able to reach this chapel, you must arm any of your wounded that are physically capable of operating a weapon. Those that are too badly injured to do so can at least reload for the others." Mary nodded her head in assent, and as she looked up at her big brother, she noticed the look of unspoken anxiety and sorrow in his eyes. "Promise me, sis," He went on, his voice breaking slightly, as he took both of her hands in his, "That you will be careful, for my sake? I won't be here to protect you, and..." His voice trailed off completely. Mary's eyes filled with tears as she reached up and wrapped her arms around her brother's neck in a sisterly embrace. "I promise, Ben." She whispered. He held her tightly, as he blinked the tears from his eyes. "God will be with both of us." He said at last. "Yes," Mary replied with emotion. "'Though we walk through the valley of the shadow of death, we shall fear no evil, for He is with us [18].'"

When the bombardments from the enemy began once again, a distinct change could be noticed in the attitudes of each of the Texan defenders. Each seemed to be resigned to their fate, and while they all appeared to be weighed down with feelings akin to despair, one could also detect a certain look in their eyes that told of a deep and burning resolve to withstand their foes with such ferocity as to make them repent that they had ever undertaken the attack.

When night fell, Travis ordered Crockett and Ben to make yet another sortie with their men. This time, they were ordered to directly attack and harass the Mexican troops in order to cause enough confusion to throw their next onslaught into disorder. This attempt was somewhat successful, as the small band of Texans quickly became the cause of much panic amongst the Mexican troops. Despite this, however, the enemy continued on with their advance, moving their guns still closer to the Alamo, and even setting up a stalwart battery in close proximity of the Alamo's north wall. By the next morning, this new battery began pounding away at the old fortress, and though it was comprised of only light field pieces, the short distance separating them from the north wall allowed for their steady fire to take serious effect [1]. All throughout the day, the incessant barrage continued, and on into the next.

By the latter part of the morning of March 5, the wall began showing signs of giving way. "I don't know how much longer that old wall is going to hold up Davy." Ben yelled to his friend over the din of the siege, as he observed the state of the said structure from his battle station. "I don't reckon it will Ben," Crockett hollered back, "And when it gives out, we"— but before he could finish his sentence, he was interrupted by a loud crashing sound, that was accompanied by a shower of broken stone and clouds of dust. Both men were struck with horror when they caught sight of a large, gaping hole that had been blown through the east part of the north wall of the Alamo. Together with many other defenders, they rushed to the spot to face the subsequent enemy advance that they knew was sure to come. "Now for the end!" Ben heard Crockett mutter to himself as they ran. "I only wish that we might take down the whole lot of them before we fall!" However, to the bewilderment of all the men, the expected attack did not come. In fact, the enemy fire began to grow lighter and lighter, until eventually, except for an occasional shell being fired over the walls or a spattering of fire from small arms, silence predominantly prevailed.

After several hours of this, Crockett got up from his position next to Ben and said, "Well lad, I've just about had enough of this waitin' nonsense. I figure the best thing to do now is set a good watch, and then get ourselves some grub and shut-eye. It's hard to tell what them varmints have got up their sleeves, but it is my opinion that they intend to catch us off guard. We might as well get rest while we can, as I'm sartain' we'll have to be on the lookout all night." "I suppose you're right, Davy," Ben replied, "For I would have thought they'd have attacked by now!" "Oh there's no fear of that," Crockett answered with a hard laugh, "It is all too clear that they wish to take us by surprise, and that is why we must be ready for them, and not let down our guard. I'm goin' to have a talk with Travis, so why don't you go after your evening rations and then spend some time with Mary? I'll ask Travis to give you the late watch tonight so that you can be with her for a good while." "Thank you, Davy," Ben replied quietly. "I would appreciate that very much."

As soon as Ben had finished his meager supper, he made his way to the old chapel to find Mary. He found her sitting quietly by a small lamp, busily occupied with tearing up a few old sheets for the use of wound dressings. Ben pulled up an empty barrel and sat down beside her. "I'm sorry that I've not come to see you sooner, Mary." He said, in response to the sunny smile she greeted him with. "Please don't trouble yourself about that Ben," She replied, "I know that the fighting has become increasingly intense over these past couple days, and has been taxing your efforts to the utmost." "That it has," Ben answered wearily. "I'm afraid the Mexican batteries managed to breach the north wall earlier today, although oddly enough, they haven't bothered to do anything about it yet." "Yes, I heard about that from one of the men. Do you think they will attack us again soon?" "It's hard to say, Mary, but Colonel Crockett believes they mean to take us by surprise, and he is going to suggest to Travis that we keep an especially vigilant watch tonight." Both siblings grew silent for several long minutes, preoccupied with their own thoughts. "I've been doing a lot of thinking today, Ben," Mary said presently, "Particularly about all the wonderful times we've had together as children." "Is that so, Mary? Which memories were you thinking of?" Ben queried curiously. "Mostly of the wonderful times our family spent together on the farm." Mary replied, a faraway look coming into her soft brown eyes. "Do you remember the very first time you took me hunting with you?" "Oh, how could I forget?" Laughed Ben. "It was when I went after the bear that killed our hogs. As I recall, you were simply terrified of being eaten up by wild animals!" "Indeed I was, being a young and foolish little thing, but I was very comforted when you gave me your hunting knife to defend myself with." "Yes! And when we returned home again, Papa insisted that if you were going to be running about with me in the woods, that you had better learn how to shoot." Ben chuckled as he uttered this last sentence. "You certainly were a fast learner!" He went on, "I'll never forget my chagrin when I realized you were a better shot than I — and ever since then, I've still not been able to best you!" "Oh Ben!" Mary exclaimed, laughing along with him. Once she had regained her composure, she eagerly continued on with her reminiscing. "I'll never forget about that young colt Papa bought when our old mare died." She said, "He was young and so very wild and fiery. Even Papa wasn't able to break him, and began thinking that the best recourse would be to shoot the brute. But you insisted on trying him yourself! Do you recall how you would take him into the corral behind the barn where mother couldn't see you, and try repeatedly to ride him?" "Yes, and at first I always got bucked off!" "But you didn't give it up, Ben, and made me promise not to tell our parents so that you could surprise them." "I think I was mostly concerned about not getting into trouble." Ben said with a sly grin. "True,"

Laughed Mary, "But once you finished breaking that colt, and rode him out in front of the house to show Papa, I know you were pleased by his response." "He said that he was very proud of me," Ben said in a low voice. "I don't think I ever felt so pleased about anything in all my life." "There was also the time when you rigged up that bear carcass in the barn to scare Papa!" Mary went on, attempting in vain to suppress her mirth, "You rigged up a pulley to the hayloft of the barn so you could raise it up and down, and make it seem more alive — remember?" "I don't believe I could forget if I tried!" Ben laughed, "But instead of Papa coming into the barn as I was expecting, it was Mama coming to collect the eggs! I didn't realize my mistake until it was too late." "Papa and I were down at the hen house getting one of the fat old birds for supper," Mary said, "We were both appalled when we heard the most terrifying shriek coming from the barn, and were even more alarmed when we heard it quickly followed by a loud yell from you!" "I couldn't help but yell when Mama charged at the bear's carcass with a pitchfork, for I was standing right behind it! And before I could get away, Mama discovered and caught me, and — well gosh, that was probably the worst licking I ever had in my life!" At this, both siblings rocked with uncontrollable laughter that caused the tears to stream down their faces.

"Those were such precious memories," Mary said at last almost sadly, as she wiped her eyes, "How I wish those times could have lasted forever." "So do I Mary." Ben replied, his gravity returning, "We certainly had some wonderful times together, didn't we?" Mary nodded, and the next instant, she had buried her face in the sheets in her lap, her shoulders shaking with her sobs. Ben felt a large lump come up in his throat, and for a moment, his vision blurred. He couldn't think of anything appropriate to say just then, so he gently passed his arm about her, and drew her closer to his side. Mary leaned her head against her big brother's strong shoulder, and gradually her sobs died away. "Mary," Ben said presently, as he carefully pressed his handkerchief into her hand, "I know the thought of... of having to be separated from each other is very painful, and in many ways unthinkable. But what has brought me great comfort is the knowledge that our Lord will sustain us through whatever lies ahead for us in the coming hours, and, if we must be parted from each other here on this earth, it will almost surely only be for a short while. Just think, Mary," He continued, almost excitedly, "We will soon see our father and mother again — can you imagine it? And once reunited in our heavenly home, we shall never be parted from each other again." "It will be far more wonderful than anything we can fathom." She replied in a somewhat muffled voice, as she wiped the tears from her eyes. "My only wish is that I could spare you from all of the pain and grief the next few hours will bring!" Ben went on with deep emotion. "I wouldn't have it any other way, Ben, you know that." Mary said softly, "And I am so glad we will be together to the end, for I don't know what I would do without you." Ben responded by resting his head caressingly against that of his sister's. "Nor I without you, sis." He answered quietly.

The occasional sound of enemy fire had now died out altogether, and Ben and Mary sat together in silence, listening to the chirping crickets, and enjoying every precious moment together. Eventually, Mary drifted off to sleep, her head still resting against her brother's shoulder. Ben remained wakeful for some time longer, pondering on all of the events that had taken place over the previous weeks, and wondering what the morning had in store for the defenders of the Alamo. He looked down at Mary, and was comforted to notice the peaceful look that rested on her countenance. "Heavenly Father," He whispered, "I thank You for giving me such a courageous little sister, and that You will be there to protect and watch over her... even when I am gone." He then bent his head low, and kissed Mary's forehead before leaning back again against the wall, and allowing the weariness he felt to pull him into a dreamless slumber.

Crockett came to wake Ben a couple of hours later when their turn at watch came. Mary also got up, and after bidding her brother a hasty farewell, she made her way to Colonel Bowie, who lay confined to his bed in the Alamo's long barracks, still too ill to get up, but insistent on remaining where he could be close to the men. After ensuring that Bowie had everything he needed, and was as comfortable as she could make him, Mary went back to the chapel to return to her regular duties. All was still inside of the old mission, for the intense stress, the constant bombardment, skirmishes, and lack of sleep had left the defenders utterly exhausted, and many of them lay sound asleep.

It was now nearing 5:00 in the morning; Ben and Colonel Crockett stood at their sentry posts, struggling to keep awake. They were too weary to even speak with each other, and occasionally paced back and forth in order to maintain their wakefulness. Suddenly, in the middle of one of his turns, Ben stopped and peered anxiously into the darkness. "Davy!" He called softly, "I think I see something stirring in the Bexar plaza!" Instantly, Crockett was at Ben's side. "You're right, lad," He exclaimed in a low voice after a moment, "It's hard to see, but there's just enough moonlight to see them movin' around over there." "Do you think they are preparing to attack?" Ben asked quickly. "I can't imagine what else they'd be doin' at this early hour," Crockett replied grimly, "We'd better notify Travis and make ready for their attack. Our men need to be as prepared as they can be!" He had hardly finished his sentence before a loud cheer erupted from the enemy quarter. "Viva Santa Anna!" "Viva Santa Anna!" Was the chilling battle cry shouted by the Mexican troops at the tops of their lungs, so loudly that the Texans in the Alamo could not help but hear them. "The enemy is upon us, boys!" Roared Crockett, "Every man to his station!" The next instant, the men heard the call of a bugle, which was followed up by shouting from the ranking officers of the Mexican army. "Here they come Davy!" Cried Ben, as he glimpsed the enemy lines beginning their advance. "This is it Ben," Came from Crockett in a cool, clear voice, "Don't throw away a shot — and remember what you're fighting for!"

Travis was at the northeast corner of the plaza, busily directing the men in charge of the cannon that had been positioned there to help protect the breach that had been made in the north wall the day before. The sounds of the infamous "Deguello" call now floated through the early morning air. "What on 'arth do that there tune mean, Colonel Travis, Sir?" One of the men next to Travis queried. "It's the Mexican army's signal for no quarter, and is a declaration of their intention to put all of their foes to a barbarous death." Travis replied in a hard tone [1], [28]. "Is that so?" the fellow replied wrathfully, "Well then, we'll just have to make 'em eat them words, and put ol' Sant' Anna's army into a good and sorry state so that 'ol Houston can knock them into oblivion!" And the other men who were gathered nearby assented heartily.

The Mexican forces had nearly closed in on the Alamo, and despite the poor lighting, every one of the Texans could now see them distinctly. Each man clutched his firearm tightly, every nerve taut, anxiously awaiting the command to open fire. At last, the order came. "Fire!" Travis bellowed, and instantly, the men opened up on the enemy troops. The Alamo's cannons also came to life, pouring their deadly charge of scrap iron and other makeshift projectiles into the enemy ranks. The din was terrific, with the roaring of the cannons, the crack of the rifles, the yells of the attackers and defenders, and shrieks from the wounded. "Why isn't Santa Anna making use of his artillery?" Ben cried above the noise to Crockett as he was reloading his rifle. "I reckon that he's scared o' hitting his own troops!" The latter hollered back, "Lucky for us!" Ben exclaimed, "If it weren't for that, I don't think we'd be able to hold out so well!"

Indeed, the Texan defenders put up such a ferocious fight that the Mexican army was unable to close in completely upon the old mission. The attack upon the breached north wall was met with such warmth and vigor that, despite any of the urgings of the commanding officers, the Mexican troops broke and fled, even trampling one of their generals to death in their flight. The assaults upon the east and west sides of the Alamo also met with the same fate, and though the Mexican troops attacking the south side were able to reach the foot of the wall to plant their scaling ladders, they too were driven off, and any foe attempting to scale the wall was quickly dispatched [1].

Almost as quickly as it had started, the fighting came to an abrupt end, as the Mexican army beat a hasty retreat, and in such a panicked state that their superiors had great difficulty getting them under control again. "Thank God!" Ben ejaculated, as he watched the disorderly mass disappear into the darkness, which was now quickly lightening up as dawn approached. "Yes indeed," Crockett replied, "It is next to a miracle that we could repulse them varmints this time, even despite the poor lightin'!" "I suppose that the next time they attack, it will be daylight." Ben remarked, as he turned away from the wall. "Quiet possibly," Crockett answered, "I don't figure they will attack again at once, since it seems to be their habit to try an' catch us nappin'." He shook his head as he uttered these last words. "Their tactics bring to mind a pack of hungry wolves stalkin' their prey and attacking just when they believe that prey to be weary an' off guard."

The next quarter of an hour was spent by several of the men in transporting the wounded to the old chapel, where Mary was busily at work. Dilapidated benches and make-shift cots served as the hospital beds, and when these ran short, Mary was forced to make up beds upon the dirty brick floor. She moved quickly and efficiently from patient to patient, binding up their wounds as best she could, and doing her best to make them as comfortable as circumstances would allow. Just as she had hoped, there were many men who had only sustained minor injuries, and were rendered well enough to return to their posts after she had tended to them.

With the coming of dawn, the defenders could see their foes quite clearly. The space separating their position from the enemy was littered with the wounded and dying. They watched as the Mexican officers moved about amongst the men, and by their gesticulations, they guessed they were doing their best to stir up the troops and goad them into a state of fury for the next attack. "There they go, musterin' up the courage to come at us agin'," One of the Texans sang out, "I reckon we'll jest have to larn 'em as we did b'fore!" The men were all at their posts by this time, tensely waiting for the attack to begin once again. Suddenly, the temporary morning stillness was interrupted by the call of the bugle, summoning the Mexican troops to advance, and at almost the same instant they charged forward once again, with often repeated cheers for, "Generalissimo Santa Anna!"

As soon as they came into range, Travis gave the order to open fire. Again, the enemy forces attempted to reach the walls of the Alamo to plant their scaling ladders, and yet again, they were met with the same heavy fire and determination as before. The northern wall was the only position at which the Mexican army could make any progress, and by sheer luck, they somehow reached the foot of it to renew their attempt to scale its face. Some of the soldiers were even thrust up and over the wall by the force and impetus of the densely backed mass of troops, but despite their efforts, the Texans once again quickly forced them back, and it wasn't long before the entire body of enemy troops were put to flight.

Ben and Colonel Crockett were stationed with the men on the north wall, and as they watched the enemy retreat, Crockett cried out, "Every man stay down behind the wall, or you'll likely become a target for the Mexican troops!" As the men made haste to take cover behind the protecting structure, Crockett turned to Ben, saying, "You see how the Mexicans are turning to look back at us, Drury? They're scared, but they're also angry, and it's clear that they hope to get a shot off at any of us as is fool enough to show hisself." Ben nodded in acknowledgement of his friend's remark, never once taking his eyes off the retreating enemy detachment. "How goes it up here, men?" The voice of Travis was heard to call loudly behind them as he mounted the wall and came to look over the state of the said bastion. "I heard that you had a rather hot time of it here, and have come to" — At that instant, Ben spotted one of the Mexicans in the rear of the retreat turn upon hearing the sound of Travis's voice, and upon seeing the Colonel's figure standing in the open, the villain quickly raised his rifle to his shoulder. Ben had not yet been able to finish reloading his weapon, and seeing his commander's danger, he did the only thing he could, which was to spring to his feet, and throw himself against Travis, shouting, "Get down, Sir!" As he did so. A loud report from a rifle rang out, and both men toppled down to the floor behind the wall. Travis, completely unconscious of the attempt made upon his life, immediately began to get to his feet again, but he was swiftly thrust down once more by Davy Crockett, and the latter quickly raised his rifle to his shoulder, and fired after the retreating figure of the brute who had discharged the treacherous shot. "That varmint won't be pullin' a trick like that again!" He muttered as he watched the man fall.

By this time, Travis had risen to one knee, his face red with his struggles and frustration. "Good heavens, man!" He exclaimed angrily to Crockett, "I must be permitted to go about my duties without any interference! You two are acting as jumpy as old women, and I" — Heedless of Travis' raging, Crockett knelt beside the motionless form of Ben, who laid as he had fallen, in a crumpled position next to the wall. Crockett gently turned him over on his back, and to his horror, he saw that his young friend's buckskin shirt was soaked with blood from a wound in his abdomen. He turned to look at the Colonel, who had quickly been rendered speechless at the sight. "That bullet was meant for you, Travis." Was all he said in a low voice. He then carefully gathered Ben's still form in his arms, and was relieved to hear him give a low groan. "Perhaps there is yet time for Miss Mary to see to him!" He said to himself as he bore Ben swiftly to the chapel.

As soon as he reached his destination, Crockett wasted no time in applying his boot to the sturdy wooden door. "Open up!" He roared, "For Heaven's sakes, open up!" A moment later, the door was flung open by one of the

Texans, who had come to the chapel shortly before with a wounded comrade. Crockett hastily pushed past him, and scanned the room for Mary. She had just finished binding up a leg wound and looked up quickly to see what had caused the commotion at the door. As soon as she caught sight of Crockett, the color drained from her face, and for a moment, he thought she might faint. However, the poor girl swiftly regained her composure, and without another word, she motioned Crockett to an empty cot, to which he quickly bore his burden. "He ain't dead, Miss Mary," the latter said reassuringly as soon as he had reached her. "He's just been rendered unconscious by the loss of blood." As soon as Ben had been gently deposited on the cot, Mary quickly tore open his shirt and began working feverishly to stop the heavy flow of blood from the wound in his abdomen. Colonel Crockett never once left her side except for when she asked him to fetch more wound dressings from her scanty stock of medical supplies. After several failed attempts, she managed at last to check the bleeding, and was then able to proceed with bandaging Ben's wound. Just as she was finishing, Ben gave a groan, and his eyes fluttered open. "Mary?" He whispered faintly, as he caught sight of her pale face, "Is it you?" "I'm here Ben," she answered gently, kneeling by his side and taking his cold hand in hers. "Colonel Crockett brought you to me." Ben turning his head slowly to see his friend's tall form, as he stood quietly behind Mary. "Thank you Davy," He said in a low, weak voice, "I thought that I might never see her again" — He was interrupted by a heavy fit of coughing, which caused blood to stain his mouth. Mary wiped it away and gave him a small drink of water. "Davy," Ben began again, faintly, "If it isn't too much trouble... could you — sort of keep an eye on Mary for me when I am gone? I know we can't last much longer here — but I can't bear the thought of there being no one to look out after her... and — you are the only man here with whom I feel at peace entrusting her to." "I'd be honored to, Ben," Crockett answered warmly, "And I'll do all that I can for her, so just you set your mind at ease." "Thank you, Davy." Ben whispered, and then, turning his ashen face once again to his sister, he said in a low, tender voice, "I must leave you now Mary. Funny, isn't it? Me going ahead of you once again to our new home in a far distant land — only this time, when we meet again, we will be reunited for eternity, without any fear of goodbyes or partings." "Oh how wonderful that reunion will be Ben!" Mary cried softly, the tears now flowing freely down her cheeks. Ben was assailed by yet another fit of coughing that caused him to grimace in pain. His breathing now came in quick, shallow gasps. "I love you Mary," He said at last, "A brother — couldn't be prouder of his little sister — than I am of you." "I love you with all of my heart Ben," Mary sobbed, bringing Ben's hand first to her lips and then resting it against her cheek, "And I am so very proud to be able to call you my brother." Ben smiled faintly and pressed her hand ever so gently. "God bless you — dear girl!" He whispered softly, and then his eyes closed, and Mary felt his grasp on her hand slowly relax. With a low cry, Mary buried her face in the cot by Ben's side and sobbed as if her heart were breaking.

Colonel Crockett quietly removed his coonskin cap, drew his sleeve across his eyes, and bowed his head. He had been mentally bracing himself for the outburst of hysterics that he expected Mary would give way to at her brother's death. However, her stifled, heart wrenching sobs did more to unnerve and move him than the expected outburst would have. For several long minutes, he stood there silently, not knowing what to do. Gradually, Mary's sobs quieted, and at last, she lifted her head slowly and strove to wipe the tears from her face. Without a word, Crockett helped her to rise to her feet, and then knelt to gather Ben's still form once more in his arms. He took him to an empty corner in the back of the chapel, where he carefully laid him down again and helped Mary to spread a thin blanket over his body.

"GOD BLESS YOU — DEAR GIRL."

There they both stood for several long moments, struggling to grasp the reality of their horrible loss. At last, Crockett turned to Mary; the tired, grief-stricken look on her pale, tear-stained face smote him to the heart. He also noted that she was trembling slightly, and seemed very unsteady on her feet. "Begging your pardon Miss Mary," He said, "But might I ask when you last had anything to eat or drink? I know that this doesn't seem like a proper time for such doings, but you look so faint, and I know you have a lot of work ahead of you." Mary passed her hand wearily across her brow. "I don't exactly know, Colonel Crockett," She said, "I've been too busy to think of such matters... but I don't recall eating anything since the morning of the last day I spent with Ben." "Why, that is over a day ago!" Crockett exclaimed in a worried voice, "You cannot go on this way Miss Mary, or you will almost certainly collapse from faintness. Won't you please allow me to take you to retrieve somethin' to eat before the next wave of attack comes?" "Oh, but my patients, Colonel, they will need me, and indeed I fear that I have spent too much time here already!" She turned back to look at the wounded men that lay about the chapel, and noticed with a slight start that still more were being brought in from the most recent assault. Crockett followed her anxious gaze, and after a moment's thought, he said, "Tell you what, Miss Mary, you go ahead and take care of those men, and I'll go and fetch something for you. When I return, I will take you somewhere for a short while where you shan't be disturbed. Remember, Miss Mary, if you do not attend to your own wellbeing, you will not be in any state to continue on with your work here." Mary bowed her head in assent. "I will do as you say, Colonel Crockett... thank you." The Colonel returned her thanks with a kind nod, and then proceeded on his errand, leaving Mary to her various tasks.

Just outside the door, he nearly bumped into Colonel Travis, who had come to the chapel to inquire after Ben. "Crockett," He exclaimed, "How is Drury? Can I see him?" "I'm afraid not, Travis," Crockett replied gravely, "He died just a short while ago." Travis started back, a look of shock and sorrow upon his face. "Dear God!" He exclaimed, "To think that I never thanked him! He was such a fine and courageous young man, far too young to die. And his poor sister... Crockett, why do you think he did it? We are all condemned men here — why would he give up his life so needlessly to save mine?" "He was a noble lad, Travis," Crockett answered simply, "In staying here, in this crumbling old fortress to fight to the end, he proved that he weren't afraid to give his life in order to give the rest of Texas a shot at a life of freedom. He also realized how much your men need their commander, and knew he couldn't just stand by and watch you get killed when there was somethin' he could do about it." He paused for a moment before continuing, "I don't remember many passages from the Good Book," He said at last, "But the one that I ain't never forgotten is about how there ain't no greater love than that of a man who'd lay down his life for a friend, and if you ask me Travis, I'd say Ben was willing to give his life because of one of the greatest kinds of love there is — the selfless, sacrificial love for his fellow man."

Footnotes:

[1] Warren, R. (1958.) *Remember the Alamo!* Random House, Inc.

[28] TSHA: Texas State Historical Association. (2020, July 20) *Degüello*. Retrieved from: https://www.tshaonline.org/handbook/entries/deguello

Chapter 8

Victory or Death

About a quarter of an hour after Crockett's conversation with Colonel Travis, he returned to the chapel for Mary with such rations as he was able to find, as well as a full water canteen that he hoped would last her for some time. As the temporary pause in the conflict showed no immediate signs of being broken, he believed it safe enough for her to leave the protecting walls of the old chapel for a few moments, and inwardly hoped that even a short reprieve from sights of death, blood, and wounded men would help to refresh her.

Without a word, Mary followed him outside, and allowed him to guide her before him to a well-sheltered corner around the backside of the chapel. However, he was still careful to keep his tall figure between her and the direction of the enemy camp until they reached their destination to shield her from any unexpected fire. Once there, he dragged over an old but sturdy barrel that happened to be in the vicinity for Mary to use as a seat. "I'm sorry that I weren't able to find you anythin' better n' salted pork and dried biscuit," He said as he gave her the food he had brought, "I know them vittles ain't particularly appetizing, but I do hope you'll try an' eat a bit so you can keep up your strength." "Thank you, Colonel Crockett." Mary replied with a weak smile, and after bowing her head to give thanks to God for her provisions, she looked back up at Crockett, who now stood with his back leaned against the wall a few paces away from her. "I cannot tell you how much I appreciate the kindness you have shown to my dear brother and I, Colonel." She said warmly, tears filling her eyes as she spoke, "Your friendship was something that neither of us were expecting when our paths were first joined together, but I assure you, it is a gift that I have not ceased to thank God for daily." "Well now, I thank you for them kind words, Miss Mary," Crockett replied, "but I know that as much as I wish it, I ain't done near as much as you make out." "Colonel Crockett," Mary said earnestly, "You've done more for us than we could ever hope to repay, and I wish there was some way I could express how grateful both Ben and I have been to you, and how much you've come to mean to us. We lost our own father when we were both very young, and well, Colonel... you've been able to take a father's place for us." At this, Crockett didn't know what to say. His gaze fell to the dirt at his feet, and for a short while, he seemed to be very preoccupied with drawing patterns in it with the toe of his boot. Finally, he coughed and cleared his throat before raising his head to meet her gaze again. "Thank you, Miss Mary." Was all that he said, but upon observing a lone tear in his eye, Mary could see that her words had touched him more than he was willing to show.

Once Mary had finished her meager rations, Crockett escorted her back to the chapel again. He went with her as far as the doorway, and then, pulling off his coonskin cap, he said, "Well, Miss Mary, I guess this is goodbye" — "Oh no, not goodbye, Colonel Crockett," Mary interjected, "Might we instead say, 'Until we meet again'? For you know that our parting here will only be temporary, and we will soon be together again in the heavenly home that our God has prepared for us." "Right you are, Miss Mary," Crockett replied, "But one thing that I want you to know is that when the enemy does finally breach our walls, and the end comes, if I'm still alive and kickin', my final stand will be made in front of this chapel." "Thank you, Colonel, that knowledge will bring great comfort to me." Mary answered quietly, offering him her hand, which he clasped tenderly. "You and your brother are two of the finest young people I've ever had the pleasure to meet," He said warmly, "And you, Miss Mary, are the bravest woman I've ever encountered, and I've been honored to know you. May God bless you, Miss!" And with a hasty bow, Colonel Crockett made his departure. He had walked only a few yards away, when he stopped and turned about to face her once more. "Until we meet again!" He called, waving his cap at her. Mary stood in the doorway for several moments, watching him go, her eyes full of tears. At last, she went back into the chapel, and resumed her duties among the wounded.

The inactivity of the Mexican army continued on for much longer than expected after the second assault, and as a result many of the Texan defenders found themselves fighting the effects of intense fatigue, being very weary from the first two waves of attack and lack of sleep. All too soon however, the watchmen caught sight of movement in the enemy quarter, and promptly roused all the men in time to prepare for the impending onslaught. Suddenly, the Mexican bugle call rang out, and with loud cheers and yells, Santa Anna's army was upon them once again. This time, however, instead of attacking fiercely on all fronts as before, they held part of their troops back, and after a brief attempt upon the east and west walls, all the Mexican troops focused their attack upon the weakened and damaged north wall. Their sheer force and number caused the small body of men defending the north wall to waver. Texans from various defensive positions rushed to join their struggling comrades in its defense, but the vast number of Mexican troops that separated them stranded many on the east and west ramparts. The Texans worked feverishly to push the enemy back, but many of the Mexican troops were so close to the walls that the Texans could not get good shots at them, and to make matters worse, the absolute torrent of heavy fire from the rear of the Mexican ranks would not permit them to stay atop the walls. Before long, the scaling ladders were in place, and the Mexicans tried to force their way over the wall. The Mexican fire was forced to slacken at this point to avoid killing their own men, giving the Texans the opportunity to go at their foes with everything they had. A bloody hand-to-hand combat ensued, and despite all odds, for a time, the Texans somehow managed to prevent the Mexican troops from getting over the wall [1].

While the vicious conflict at the north wall continued, the enemy reached the south wall and attempted to force their way over that position as well. However, they were stoutly resisted and obstructed from their purpose by the few Texans stationed there. Finally, the Mexican troops closed in upon the west wall, which was poorly defended, as many of the Texans had left to join their companions on the north wall. Those who were still positioned at the west wall fought as hard as they could, but there were simply not enough men to hold the enemy back. Despite the valiant efforts of the Texans, the Mexican troops forced their way over the wall and into the Alamo, until at last it was completely overwhelmed, and those of the enemy that had forced their way into the old fortress now attacked the main body of Texans from the rear. This new onslaught forced the Texans defending the north wall to pull back to find new defensive positions, which allowed for the Mexican troops to pour over the wall and through the breach unimpeded. Here, Colonel Travis was killed by an enemy bullet as he bravely rallied his men about one of their cannons in a last, desperate attempt to defend the north wall.

All hell seemed to break loose as the enemy swarmed about the inside of the old mission, thirsting savagely for the blood of her defenders. The carnage was horrific. The Texans were unable to regroup, and as a result, were forced to make their last stand wherever they could, or were simply cut down and trampled underfoot by their attackers. Before long, the Mexican soldiers forced their way into the long barracks, and discovered Jim Bowie, who still lay in his sickbed in his quarters. Determined to fight to the end, even in his weak condition, Bowie had armed himself with two pistols and his famous Bowie knife, and vanquished several of his ruthless foes before he himself was killed. The brutal slaughter continued unabated throughout the Alamo, as the enemy continued its relentless hunt through the old mission for its defenders. The Texans sold their lives dearly, taking down dozens of their foes before they were at last killed themselves. They made the enemy pay dearly for every square inch that they were able to take, taking up positions in every room and every corner, and before long, the place was filled with the dead bodies of the enemy. Still, Santa Anna's henchmen came on, until at last only the body of Tennesseans headed by Colonel Davy Crockett remained, standing firmly in defense of the chapel that held all the wounded, women, and children [1]. "Give them everything you've got, boys!" The Colonel cried to his men, a fiery light in his eyes, as he discharged his rifle into the mass of enemy troops as rapidly as he could reload it. The

Tennesseans put up a ferocious defense, but all too soon, the sheer force and number of Santa Anna's men overwhelmed their small band. A fierce hand-to-hand fight resulted, with the Tennesseans resorting to using their rifles as clubs to beat back their foes. Courageously, they fought with every ounce of strength they had left, beating down many of the enemy, as one by one, they finally fell before the old chapel's double doors.

Inside the chapel, Mary had kept on with her work in a feverish haste, as more wounded continued to arrive, many of whom were so gravely injured that she was often overwhelmed in her efforts to tend to them all. Once the Mexican army successfully managed to breach the Alamo's defenses and flood over its walls, several of the defenders had instructed her to bar the chapel's thick wooded doors closed to keep the enemy from gaining easy entrance. After the doors were closed, Mary could hear the sounds of the conflict outside growing louder and louder with each moment, and paused occasionally to observe the battle through one of the Alamo's heavily barred windows, which were situated at the front of the old fortress on either side of the thick wooden doors. When at last she witnessed the Tennesseans gathering before the old chapel for their final stand, she realized that the end for the Texan defenders was drawing near. She then made haste to load the rifles that Ben had supplied her with, and after setting aside one for her personal use, she began distributing the others to such of the wounded men as were well enough to use them. "Oh Miss!" One man cried when he realized what her intensions were, "Please, for our sakes, leave us and take refuge with the other women and children. We cannot bear that you should throw your life away needlessly — you have done all that you can for us now, and we are forever grateful to you!" The other men heartily assented with the speaker, also urging Mary to take shelter. "My brave fellows," Cried Mary, clasping her hands, "Though nothing I can do will save you, I cannot in good conscience retire to safety and leave you here to be slaughtered. Indeed death is a far brighter prospect to me than a life knowing that I deserted you. But I do not fear death, for I know that I will simply wake in the arms of my Savior. He gave His life for me, and for you also, even though we are all miserable, helpless sinners, fully deserving of death. None of us who have repented of our sins, and committed our lives to Him need fear death, for because of His sacrifice, we can rest assured in the promise of a life in eternity, with our Lord." She paused for a moment, and looked about the room. "Might I pray with you all, while there is yet time?" She queried earnestly. To this, the men eagerly assented, and Mary knelt in the midst of them all, and as they each bowed their heads, she began to pray. She committed each of their souls into the hands of their Creator, asking for His strength to face their end without fear, and beseeching mercy for any who had not yet turned to Him. "And may the stand of these brave men here," she prayed, "Not be in vain, and may the day soon arrive in which the people of Texas are permitted to enjoy the priceless gift of freedom that these courageous souls have sacrificed so much to give them. All this I humbly ask in the name of our Savior and Lord, Jesus Christ, Amen."

There was hardly a dry eye in the room as Mary rose from her knees. As she walked back to her post at one of the Alamo's windows to reassess their situation, many of the men reached up to gently press her hand. "God bless you, Miss Mary!", "God bless you, and thank you!" were some of the heart-felt parting words they imparted to her. "God be with you all," She exclaimed, "And may you all find peace and true freedom in our Lord!" All at once, the sounds of battle grew tenfold, and Mary, upon peering cautiously out of her window, saw with a thrill of horror that the enemy forces had nearly cleared the entire area before the old chapel, saving for a small remnant before the doorway. "They are upon us!" she cried, taking up her rifle, and positioning herself someway back from the door, upon which blows were now already heard to be raining heavily.

Footnotes:

[1] Warren, R. (1958.) *Remember the Alamo!* Random House, Inc.

"THEY ARE UPON US!" SHE CRIED, TAKING UP HER RIFLE

Chapter 9

Worth Dying For

"Beggin' your pardon, Sir, but there is a Mrs. Dickinson here to see you." "Mrs. Dickinson? Who is she?" inquired the middle-aged, white-haired gentleman who had been addressed. "She and her husband, Captain Dickinson, were stationed at San Antonio de Bexar, and she says that she has a message for you." "Indeed! Please show her in, Sergeant!" Exclaimed Doctor Dopkins, for such the gentleman was. He rose from the cot he had been reclining on as he spoke, one of the sole pieces of furniture that adorned his humble quarters, which were situated in the officer's division in the camp of General Houston's army.

The news of the massacre of the 180 odd defenders of Alamo had spread like wildfire all over Texas, filling the hearts of the Texans with dismay and outrage. To further add to their grief and turmoil, on March 19, the Texan forces under command of Colonel James Fannin were trapped by Mexican General Jose Urrea and his army while attempting to retreat from Goliad. Though surrounded by their foes, Fannin and his men had engaged in a desperate battle with Urrea's army, but were completely overwhelmed by the greatly superior enemy forces. After a long and hopeless fight, Fannin was forced to surrender on March 20, after receiving the enemy's promise that he and his men would be treated as prisoners of war, and their wounded cared for. Fannin and his men were then made prisoners and escorted to the Presidio La Bahia [12], a Mexican fortress located outside of Goliad [13]. When Santa Anna heard the news of the capture of the Texans, he ordered General Urrea to put all of them to the sword. Urrea tried to remonstrate against Santa Anna's horrific order, but his efforts proved to be worse than useless when Santa Anna sent his personal aid to Goliad to ensure that his brutal order was carried out. Tragically, on Palm Sunday, March 27, 1836, the Texan prisoners were marched out of their prison and ruthlessly shot down and bayonetted to death, while any wounded Texan captives were mercilessly executed as they lay helpless on their sickbeds. Nearly all of the 350 Texans, including Fannin, perished on that terrible day, which quickly became known throughout Texas as the Goliad Massacre [3], [20], [21], [22], [23].

The tragic events of the past few months had told heavily on Dr. Dopkins. His silvery gray hair was now white, and his face looked older and more grave than it had when he had parted from the Drury siblings. Ever since word had arrived regarding the fall of the Alamo, he had made many inquiries in an attempt to ascertain the fate of Mary and her brother, but had been unable to learn anything. How he hoped that perhaps they had found a way to escape, or had even been miraculously spared! However, as the weeks passed, and still no word came of them, he began to fear the worst.

Before the announcement of his visitor, the doctor had been busily occupied with the inspection of his medical instruments, a task which only a few months before had been so neatly and efficiently completed by the hands of Mary Drury. Rousing himself from his musings, he quickly replaced the instruments in their cases again as the sergeant stepped back to motion the visiter into the tent. The next instant, Susanna Dickinson entered and came to stand before the doctor. "Mrs. Dickinson, what an unexpected pleasure," Doctor Dopkins began, advancing to greet her, but when he beheld her haggard, grief-stricken countenance, his voice faltered, and the color drained from his face. "Good afternoon, Doctor," Suzanna said in low, sorrow-filled tones, her eyes filling with tears. "I am afraid that I am the bearer of... of very bad tidings." She paused for a moment and pulled a small missive out of her skirt pocket. "I was a very close friend of Mary Drury, and have come here to deliver this letter that she wrote to you, as she requested me." So speaking, she handed him the note in question. "I believe Mary was once your assistant, Doctor?" She asked as she did so, solemnly observing Doctor Dopkins as he stood as if transfixed, gazing down at the letter in his hand. "Yes — yes she was, Ma'am," He said at last, looking up. "Please, can you tell me what has become of her? I have neither seen or heard of her since the day that I left her with her brother Ben in San Antonio. That was some months ago now, and I have feared the worst ever since I heard the news of what befell the Texans at the Alamo." "I have come from the Alamo myself, Sir." Suzanna said, her voice full of anguish, "Indeed I am one of the few non-combatants who survived." "Then Mary" — "It is all too true, Sir. She and her brother are both dead. They were butchered by the enemy, along with all the other courageous men who attempted to defend the Alamo. None were spared, saving us women folk and our children, for Santa Anna graciously ordered that we were not to be harmed so that we might spread the news concerning the utter slaughter he committed, hoping it would strike fear into your hearts and cause the rest of Texas to give up fighting, and surrender to him."

Doctor Dopkins sank down upon the cot, his head in his hands, too overcome at the moment to say a word. Suzanna walked over to a small trunk at the foot of the cot, and seated herself wearily, waiting patiently until the doctor was ready to talk again. "How did she die, Mrs. Dickinson?" He queried at last, without raising his head, "And why — why would they do such a thing to a young woman?" "She insisted upon staying with the wounded men under her care to the end." Suzanna answered brokenly. "Her brother and many others urged her to hide away in safety with the women and children, but she refused. She said that she just couldn't live with herself if she left them to — to be slaughtered." Suzanna paused to take a deep breath before continuing on. "After the fighting had come to an end, the Mexican troops discovered our hiding place in the back room of the Alamo's small chapel. The chapel was also where Mary had set up her hospital, and when the troops escorted us out to the large courtyard to stand before General Santa Anna, despite all of my efforts, I could not get any glimpse of her. I tried to stop and ask about her, but our captors would not permit us to speak, and hurried us along on our way. When we reached Santa Anna, I demanded to know what had become of Mary, describing her, stating where she had last been, and insisting that she be found and brought to safety. Santa Anna seemed annoyed, but he asked the officer in charge of us if he had seen the woman I described. The officer seemed rather put out by the question, and after much urging, he at last admitted that he and his men had seen Mary. He stated that during the battle, when they reached the old chapel and battered down the door, they were met with such heated fire from those inside that they were forced to get away from the doorway again, and fired volley after volley through it from a safe distance. When they at last went in again to finish their brutal work, they discovered the body of a woman lying a short distance from the door... and he said she was still clutching her rifle. When he heard this, Santa Anna condescended to tell me that he did not usually order the execution of women and children, but as Mary had actively taken part in rebellion against the Mexican government, she brought her fate upon herself, and that as a traitor, she had rightly been meted, though unintentionally, a traitor's fate."

Suzanna grew quiet for several long moments, overwhelmed by her emotions. "Oh, but it was horrible, Doctor! No matter how hard I tried, I couldn't block out the terrible sounds of our men being butchered. I think I will carry their cries to my grave, if they do not succeed in driving me mad before then! And that wasn't even the worst of it... when we were leaving, we saw the large stacks of our dead going up in flames, including the body of my dear husband — and all by the order of Santa Anna himself." The poor girl was now sobbing so hard that she could hardly speak. "I don't know how I will ever be able to go on now, Doctor Dopkins!" She cried, "The intense noise, the sounds of fighting and the groans of dying men, the smell of blood and burning bodies — sometimes I don't think that I can stand it any longer!" Susanna Dickinson covered her face with her hands, sobs wracking her frame.

Doctor Dopkins arose to his feet and walked over to the weeping young woman. "My dear Mrs. Dickinson," he said at last in a broken voice, "Only God truly knows how much you suffer. I wish that there was something that I could say to comfort you, or something that I could do to help..." Gradually, Suzanna's sobbing quieted, until at last she raised her tear-stained face to look back up at the doctor, who then gently offered her his handkerchief. "There is one source of comfort that has sustained me, Doctor Dopkins." She said as she took it from him and attempted to wipe away her tears. "When we were in that time-worn old mission, surrounded on all sides by the Mexican army, I frequently expressed the fears I had about our fate to Mary. Something that she would always tell me was that no matter what might occur, God would be our refuge and our strength [5], and that He would be always be with us." Suzanna shook her head as she went on, the tears coursing freely once again down her face. "She was right, Doctor," she exclaimed, "All throughout those terrible days, when I felt like giving way to despair, He was always there for me to turn to, and granting me such comfort as only He can give!" "Indeed, Mrs. Dickinson," Doctor Dopkins said, "Our Lord is, 'A father of the fatherless, a defender of widows [9].' It brings me such joy to hear that our dear Mary was able to speak words of comfort to you in your hour of need." "She was a treasure Doctor, and I am so blessed to have known her." Suzanna replied with conviction.

Doctor Dopkins now turned his attention to the letter from Mary that Suzanna had given to him. "When did she write this?" He queried. "It was on the day that Travis received word that there would be no help coming to us, and we realized the impossibility of the Alamo being able to withstand Santa Anna." Suzanna replied, "She brought it to me that evening, and asked me to try and get it to you if I survived." For a while, the doctor just gazed at the letter, turning it over and over in his hands. At last, he walked back to his cot, and putting on his spectacles, he sat down and began to read. He was so long over it that Suzanna started to wonder if she had better take her leave, but just as she was about to rise, Doctor Dopkins looked up again. "Mrs. Dickinson," He said, "I think I will read this letter to you. If it were possible, I would read it to all of Texas, for in it is something that is vitally important for us as free Texans to remember as we continue on in our struggle for liberty — namely, what the true purpose of our stand is for." He paused momentarily before adding, "I hope and pray that the ultimate sacrifice so many willingly made to allow for others to enjoy a life of freedom will never be forgotten. And may we never falter in our cause to secure the precious gift for which they gave their lives to attain, that their sacrifice might not be squandered." As he uttered these last words, the doctor once again returned his gaze to the letter in his hand, and after he had cleared his throat, and adjusted his glasses, he began to read aloud:

March 3, 1836,
The Alamo

My dear Doctor Dopkins, The Alamo

Doubtless, by the time that this letter reaches you, you will have heard word of the fate that has befallen the defenders of the Alamo.

I want you to know how deeply grateful I am to you for everything that you have taught me, for it is because of you that I now have the ability to help the wounded men here who would otherwise be left unattended. Thank you for all of the generosity and kindness that you showed to both Ben and me, and please try not to feel too badly for us, dear friend, when you learn of what has happened.

In some ways, I don't think either of us could be more satisfied with our situation than we are right now. Both Ben and I are working together to the very best of our abilities to do our duty to our God and to our fellow men by defending our beautiful land. God willing, the day will soon arrive in which there will be freedom for all of Texas.

*It is true that we are making a stand in defense of our own rights, but we are also fighting for yet another reason that is of even greater importance than this — that the generations of Texans to come may enjoy a life of true freedom, without any fear of oppression or tyranny. Regardless of what the cost to us might be Doctor Dopkins, or if we are not permitted to live to see that day, that knowledge is what makes this struggle a cause that is truly **worth dying for**.*

May our Lord always preserve and bless you,

With warmest regards,
Mary Drury

The End

Footnotes:

[5] (New King James Version, 1996, Psalm 46:1)

[9] (New King James Version, 1996, Psalm 68:5)

[12] TheAlamo.org. (n.d). *Battle and Revolution: Freedoms Worth Fighting For.* Retrieved from: https://www.thealamo.org/remember/battle-and-revolution

[13] THC: Texas Historical Commission. (n.d.) *The Presidio La Bahia State Historic Site.* Retrieved from: https://texastimetravel.com/directory/presidio-la-bahia-state-historic-site/

[20] Klein, Christopher. (2023, May 17.) *The Goliad Massacre — The Other Alamo.* Retrieved from: https://www.history.com/news/the-goliad-massacre-the-other-alamo

[21] Ron Soodalter (n.d.) *Goliad: The Bloodiest Massacre of the Texan Revolution.* Retrieved from: https://www.historynet.com/goliad-texas/

[22] Pennybacker, A. (1908) *A History of Texas, Revised.* Mrs. Percy V. Pennybacker Publisher.

[23] Steen, R. (1939) *History of Texas.* The Steck Company Publishers.

Epilogue

The sacrifice of the Texans who gave their lives at the battle of the Alamo was not in vain, for it was their brave stand that granted Houston valuable time to rally and prepare the Texan army to face Santa Anna. It also gave the Texas delegation in Washington-on-the-Brazos the time it needed to declare independence from Mexico, and inspired and rallied Texans across the nation to the cause of freedom like never before [24].

Santa Anna believed that his brutal show of force at the both the Battle of the Alamo and Goliad Massacre would strike fear into the hearts of the Texans, and presumed that his army would have no trouble annihilating that of his rag-tag rebel opponents. Little did he know how the murderous actions he had committed and hoped would wreak terror upon the Texan army would now come to work against him. On April 20, 1836, the Mexican forces finally caught up with and cornered Houston's army at the San Jacinto river [4]. The news of the slaughter of their comrades had kindled a righteous fury and burning resolve in the hearts of the Texans, which, in the end, would make their smaller force practically unstoppable. On April 21, 1836, Sam Houston and his Texans attacked Santa Anna and his much larger army during what became known as the Battle of San Jacinto [12]. With, *"Remember the Alamo"* and *"Remember Goliad"* as their battle cries, the righteous fury of the Texans was worked up to such a fever heat that not only did their significantly smaller army put their foes to flight in a mere eighteen minutes, but their victory was so decisive as to force Santa Anna (who eventually was captured on the following day) to sign a peace treaty that granted independence to all of Texas [4]. Thus, the Republic of Texas was at last firmly established [12], and though their troubles were not completely over, the Texans could now live as a free people, and eventually, in 1846, Texas would become a proud state of the United States of America [14].

The history of the Texas war for Independence and the Battle of the Alamo are an incredible chapter in America's history. From it, we learn of how a small number of freedom loving individuals were willing to give their all to stand against tyranny and oppression, and how despite overwhelming and seemingly impossible odds, they were at last able to triumph and become a free people. Though it cost them numerous untold hardships, and in many cases their very lives, these brave men valued freedom and their God-given rights (which no man on earth has the right to subvert) more than a life of "security" and relative tranquility and safety that would require an abject submission to tyranny.

Though several of the characters in this story are fictitious, there were many real life individuals just like them all throughout the history of our great country who willingly gave their all to preserve freedom for the next generation. The fight is far from being over, for it now rests upon us, the American people, to determine if these same freedoms will be passed on to our children and grandchildren. That is why each and every one of us must do our part to stand against any attempts to subvert or take away our God-given rights, be these attacks from foreign or domestic foes.

Something that many people in our day often forget is that in time, every one of us will have to answer to God for the actions that he or she has, *or has not taken,* here on this earth. As American citizens, we have a duty to honor those who sacrificed so much for our freedom. To truly honor their sacrifice and earn the precious heritage and gift of freedom they have passed on to us, we must seek to do all within our power to preserve them for the next generation. Our children are a precious gift that God has entrusted to our care, and we are responsible not only for shaping their character, and raising them to be honorable, responsible citizens, but also for safeguarding and defending the heritage and freedoms we have been given to pass on to them and their children.

Regardless of how overwhelming, wearying, or even hopeless this responsibility might seem at times, may we take heart in remembering the courageous sacrifices of those who have gone before us, and always strive to fulfill our duty to God, our country, and our families, and humbly entrust the results to God [11]. As was so truly stated by Reverend Matthias Burnett,

"Finally, ye Freemen… in whose power it is to save or destroy your country, consider well the important trust… which God… has put into your hands. To God and posterity you are accountable for them… Let not your children have reason to curse you for giving up those rights, and prostrating those institutions which our fathers delivered to you [7]."

"We view ourselves on the eve of battle. We are nerved for the contest, and must conquer or perish. It is vain to look for present aid: none is at hand. We must now act or abandon all hope! Rally to the standard, and be no longer the scoff of mercenary tongues! **Be men, be free men, that your children may bless their father's name** *[15]."*

~ Sam Houston's address to the Texans before the Battle of San Jacinto

Footnotes

[1] Warren, R. (1958.) *Remember the Alamo!* Random House, Inc.

[2] D'Souza, D. (2014.) *America: Imagine A World Without Her.* Regnery Publishing.

[3] Federer, B. (2022, February 24.) *"Remember the Alamo-Remember Goliad": History of New Spain & Texas Independence-American Minute with Bill Federer.* Retrieved from: https://americanminute.com/blogs/todays-american-minute/remember-the-alamo-remember-goliad-history-of-new-spain-texas-american-minute-with-bill-federer

[4] Giorello, J. (2016.) *Bunker Hill to WWI: Great Battles for Boys.* Rolling Wheel Publishing.

[5] (New King James Version, 1996, Psalm 46:1)

[6] The Alamo. (n.d.) *Travis Letter: Victory or Death.* Retrieved from: https://www.thealamo.org/remember/battle-and-revolution/travis-letter

[7] National Black Robe Regiment. (2014, March 11) *An ELECTION SERMON, Preached by Matthias Burnet.* Retrieved from: *https://nationalblackroberegiment.com/sermon-election-1803/*

[8] Overall Motivation. (n.d.) *Ronald Reagan Quotes On Freedom, Socialism, Communism.* Retrieved from: https://www.overallmotivation.com/quotes/ronald-reagan-quotes-freedom-socialism-communism/

[9] (New King James Version, 1996, Psalm 68:5)

[10] Minster, Christopher. (2020, August 28). Timeline of the Texas Revolution. Retrieved from: https://www.thoughtco.com/important-dates-in-texas-independence-2136254

[11] Barry, S. (n.d.) *"Duty is ours, results are God's"* Retrieved from: https://www.patriotacademy.com/duty-is-ours-results-are-gods/

[12] TheAlamo.org. (n.d). *Battle and Revolution: Freedoms Worth Fighting For.* Retrieved from: https://www.thealamo.org/remember/battle-and-revolution

[13] THC: Texas Historical Commission. (n.d.) *The Presidio La Bahia State Historic Site*. Retrieved from: https://texastimetravel.com/directory/presidio-la-bahia-state-historic-site/

[14] Winders, B. (n.d). *July 4th: Independence and Annexation*. Retrieved from: https://www.thealamo.org/remember/military-occupation/independence-and-annexation

[15] SJM: San Jacinto Museum and Battlefield. (n.d.) *Sam Houston: General, led Texians to victory at San Jacinto*. Retrieved from: https://www.sanjacinto-museum.org/Discover/The_Battle/Commanders/Sam_Houston/

[16] BrainyQuote.com. (n.d.). *John Wayne Quotes*. Retrieved from: https://www.brainyquote.com/quotes/john_wayne_664751

[17] Nevada Technical Associates. (n.d.) *William Barret Travis — Alamo Letters*. Retrieved from: https://www.ntanet.net/travis.html

[18] (New King James Version, 1996, Psalm 23:4)

[19] TheAlamo.org. (n.d). *Heroes Who Died Fighting for Freedom*. Retrieved from: https://www.thealamo.org/remember/battle-and-revolution/defenders#sortByName

[20] Klein, Christopher. (2023, May 17.) *The Goliad Massacre — The Other Alamo*. Retrieved from: https://www.history.com/news/the-goliad-massacre-the-other-alamo

[21] Ron Soodalter (n.d.) *Goliad: The Bloodiest Massacre of the Texan Revolution*. Retrieved from: https://www.historynet.com/goliad-texas/

[22] Pennybacker, A. (1908) *A History of Texas, Revised*. Mrs. Percy V. Pennybacker Publisher.

[23] Steen, R. (1939) *History of Texas*. The Steck Company Publishers.

[24] Barker, E., & Pohl, J. (2024, March 7). *Texas Revolution*. Retrieved from: https://www.tshaonline.org/handbook/entries/texas-revolution

[25] Hardeman, L. (2020, December 7). *Goliad Campaign of 1835*. Retrieved from: https://texasproud.com/texas-goliad-campaign-of-1835/

[26] TheAlamo.org. (n.d.) *The Importance of Béxar and the Alamo in the Texas Revolution.* Retrieved from: https://www.thealamo.org/remember/battle-and-revolution/bexar

[27] Captivating History. (2020) *History of Texas.* Captivating History

[28] TSHA: Texas State Historical Association. (2020, July 20) *Degüello.* Retrieved from: https://www.tshaonline.org/handbook/entries/deguello